CHRISTMAS MURDER IN HYANNIS

Utterly Addictive Cozy Mystery

MASSACHUSETTS COZY MYSTERY
Book 4

ANDREA KRESS

© 2023

Chapter 1

1933

IT'S A STRANGE, yet satisfying phenomenon, that a close friendship formed early in life, even after a long separation, can resume later as if no time had elapsed. Amanda Burnside smiled to herself, recognizing that she and her old school friend, Kitty Warren, fell into just such a category. They met in elementary school and were an odd two-some: Amanda, tall and thin with a light brown bob, and Kitty, a petite girl with dark hair in braids. Later their paths diverged—Amanda became a day student at one of Boston's best schools for girls —while Kitty was sent out west due to her more delicate health. The Warren family relocated for a while but recently had come back to Boston. Now in their early twenties, Amanda and Kitty reconnected with the same joy and laughter they had once shared. With both of them in Beacon Hill, they vowed to keep in close touch.

Amanda was starting her day having breakfast with her parents prior to going to her job at Mercy Hospital where she coordinated the locations of clinics for indigent children. With two sites established so far, she was working on where the next one could go and was deep in thought as she sat at the table.

"You'll get wrinkles scowling like that," her mother scolded with a smile.

"What do you think happened to me?" her father said. "It's not just old age, it's worry."

"You're not old and I thought Mother was the one who worried."

"She worries about home and family issues. I get to agonize about work."

"What is there to be worried about at work?" Amanda asked, taking a piece of toast from the rack. Her father rarely talked about his business as a partner at a prestigious law firm.

"What all managers are troubled by. Their employees."

"I should think that people would be happy to have work in these difficult economic times," Mrs. Burnside said.

"That's just it. Our investigator hasn't come into work for the past two days due to illness."

"Surely that can't be helped. And if it's contagious, you wouldn't want him coming in anyway."

"He has asthma, a chronic condition that gets worse as the weather gets colder. I spoke to him on the telephone, and he was wheezing audibly. I can assure you, he wasn't making it up because he's had these episodes before. It's still an inconvenience as his work is piling up in the meantime."

There was a distant ringing of the telephone and Simona, one of the maids, came in shortly thereafter.

"Excuse me, Miss, but the call is for you."

Amanda got up cheerfully, expecting it to be her boyfriend, Brendan Halloran, but she came back to the table several minutes later with a look of shock on her face.

"Who was it?" her mother asked.

"Mr. Barlow."

"How odd for your boss to call for you at home. You are going to work today, aren't you?"

"He's leaving the hospital. He's accepted a job somewhere else." Amanda slumped into her seat.

"Oh, dear. You rather liked him, didn't you?"

"Yes, he is so organized and forward thinking."

"A shame that he's leaving," Mr. Burnside said. "But there's always change in the work world, you know," he advised.

"The trouble is, just now he offered me a job working for him at his new position."

"How lovely," Mrs. Burnside said.

"At a hospital in Hartford, Connecticut," Amanda offered.

Her mother put her fork down and looked over at her husband, who was trying hard to show no reaction.

"That's quite an honor," he said.

"What are you going to do?" her mother asked.

Amanda looked at her parents. "Well, first, I think I'll eat my breakfast."

That got a forced laugh from them until they realized she hadn't entirely absorbed the news yet herself. She mechanically spread jelly on toast and took a bite but had no impression of what it tasted like.

What did this all mean? What would happen to the clinic project? Would the job she was doing now cease to exist once Mr. Barlow left since he had been the one to champion it in the first place? Who would step into his place? Although Hartford wasn't that far away, could she even think of leaving her family and relocating? And what about her relationship with Brendan?

They ate in silence for a few minutes more.

"Lots of decisions to be made," Mr. Burnside said.

"About what?" asked Louisa, the younger daughter finally coming down for the first meal of the day.

"Work," Amanda and Mr. Burnside answered simultaneously.

Louisa shook her head as if not understanding what they were talking about. "Speaking of work, Daddy, you'll never guess."

He looked up suspiciously from his plate. "Work? You?"

"Don't be such a tease. I know you think that clothing design course I've been taking was a frivolous waste of time just to keep me occupied." By which she meant out of the sphere of her boyfriend, Rob Worley, a nightclub owner who likely dabbled in other shady enterprises. "But Monsieur Josef saw my sketches and, of course, noticed my own wardrobe and has agreed to take me on as an apprentice designer."

"That's wonderful," Mrs. Burnside said, eager to have her doing anything but sitting at home all day to save up energy for her nights at the club. She also recognized the name of the man who had a salon that catered to the rich and fashionable.

"I'm rather pleased," Louisa said with a smug smile.

"You always did have an eye for color and flair," her mother said.

"Don't go running off to New York. Or Paris, now," her father said but none of them knew if he were being serious.

"Not yet, Daddy, not yet."

They resumed eating and the telephone rang again. Simona entered the breakfast room again. "Excuse me, Miss, but the call is for you."

"Again?" her father asked.

Amanda was gone a while for this call and her mother fretted that it could be some other complication in her work or personal life. She returned looking ashen.

"What is it?"

"Kitty Warren. Her father was found dead at their beach house in Hyannis."

Chapter 2

Amanda was going to Kitty's home shortly, but first it was necessary to call Brendan and tell him the morning's news.

"I'm sorry to hear about Kitty's father, sweetheart," he said.

"Oh, Bren, I don't have any details but I'm sure someone will fill me in. I won't be going in to work today. And work—I haven't told you about Mr. Barlow." She proceeded to relate the brief conversation she had had with the Director of the hospital and when she got to the part of his offering her a job, Brendan fell silent.

"That's a feather in your cap, I suppose," he said.

"Yes, I'm flattered, but I don't want to face him or make a decision today."

"I hope that has something to do with me."

"Of course. Don't be ridiculous. You're a part of all my decisions these days as you well know."

"That doesn't tell me whether you are considering his offer or not."

"I just got it a half hour ago. I hadn't had time to think about it. And then Kitty called."

"I'll let you go and tend to your friend. Please pass on my condolences. And call me later. I want to make sure you're all right."

Amanda hung up the telephone and inhaled deeply. This was going to be a difficult day.

Kitty lived three blocks away and, although the weather was nippy, Amanda thought it a good idea to walk to clear her head. The trees were bare and random leaves swirled around her feet in eddies of wind gusts that made her pull her coat more closely to her neck. December and gray skies seemed to go together, and it would be like this until late March. The weather had to be much colder and rawer on Cape Cod and she wondered what Mr. Warren had been doing out there. It was chiefly their summer house, not unlike her own family's beach house in Maine except much grander. Hyannis homes along the water were full-sized houses built back from the beach to allow for a copious lawn where families played croquet and could be observed by others seated on the terrace in the shade. Several families shared a dock where small sailboats were tied for short forays into the bay, but those would have been put into storage already as no one would dare sail with the potential of winter storms. Amanda remembered the Warrens' house, Belvedere, consisted of a wall of windows that looked out over the water—a wonderful feature that could mean a drafty place in cold weather. She shivered at the thought and once again wondered what Mr. Warren had been doing out there. Locking up the place for winter? Wouldn't that have been done months ago?

There was already a black wreath on the Warrens' front door when Amanda rang the bell. A maid answered and recognizing her showed her into the study where Kitty sat in front of an open picture album.

They flew into each other's arms. Kitty sobbed and Amanda cried.

"How sorry am I for you and your mother. What can I do to help?" Amanda asked, knowing once the words were out of her mouth that her question was too vague for an answer. She took her coat and hat off and they both sat on the sofa.

"I was just looking at these," Kitty said, motioning to family photographs mounted on the thick black pages of an album, some of whose chevron-shaped corner holders had come unglued, setting a few snaps askew. Kitty pushed those back into position. "Do you remember that funny man who had a farm out in Belmont and you could ride his impossibly tame horses around the corral?"

"Oh, yes. They were huge and moved so slowly but we thought we were practically racing. I'll bet they hadn't trotted in years. Is that where that was taken?" Amanda asked, seeing a small version of Kitty on a large horse, squinting into the sun.

"I shouldn't be looking at these now, they're just making me sad." Kitty closed the album.

"How is your mother doing?"

"She's upstairs resting."

Amanda took Kitty's hand. "When did this happen?"

Kitty exhaled to pluck up her courage. "He went down to the Cape two days ago. The house was pretty much closed up already, but he wanted to meet with the housekeeper and Josiah, the gardener. They both stop in periodically to check on things. You know, to make sure a pipe hasn't burst, or a raccoon gotten into the attic. He was supposed to come back yesterday and when he didn't, Mother got worried. And then she got a call from Gertrude who was barely coherent."

"You don't have to go on," Amanda said, sorry she had prompted the recollection.

"No, let me say it. I'll have to be saying it to people again and again. The housekeeper had already called the police who took the phone from her and explained to Mother that he was found inside the front door. He must have had a heart attack." She began to cry again.

The maid who had let Amanda in put her head around the door. "Miss? Your mother wants you."

Kitty got up slowly as if her legs were too heavy to carry her across the room.

"Do you want me to stay? Is there anything I can do to help?"

"No. Not just now, thank you."

Amanda stood and gave her another hug. "I'll call later, all right?" she said to her friend's retreating back before picking up her coat and hat and heading home.

Brendan was waiting for her in the sitting room when she returned, an unexpected visit.

He stood, took her hand, and then embraced her warmly.

"I'm so sorry," he said, which got her crying again.

"Poor Kitty," she said and led him to the sofa and sat. "I didn't know her father well. He traveled quite a bit, so I hardly saw him and then she and I ended up at different schools."

"I remember you told me you had a gap in your friendship."

"He died down at their house in Hyannis."

"Odd time of year to be down at the Cape," Brendan said.

"I don't know if they expect her mother to go down there to retrieve him, or what."

"It depends upon the circumstances. I'm assuming it was a natural death."

"That's what Kitty said."

"It would be more considerate if the sheriff's office were to arrange for transport back for him rather than have the family go down there. Here in Boston, we usually have family identify the body, but if he was well known in the community there, they wouldn't need his wife to travel down to do it."

"Let's hope. Do you know anybody in the sheriff's office to smooth the way?"

"I'm afraid not. I've been to the Cape many times but just for vacations, not in any official capacity."

They sat quietly for a few minutes.

"I'm sorry, Bren. Would you like some coffee or tea?"

"That would be nice."

"Come with me to the kitchen. Maybe Simona is in there."

She led the way but only found Cook, seated at the large butcher block counter leafing through a cookbook, reading glasses perched low on her nose.

"Hello," Brendan said, extending his hand and introducing himself.

Cook reacted with surprise. Guests didn't usually come into the kitchen, much less want to meet the help.

"He's the one who found Simona for us," Amanda said.

"Well…," Brendan corrected, knowing that it might have been his connection to the maid's family that brought her into their sphere, but it was Amanda's doing that got her the job.

"I thought I'd make some coffee," Amanda said.

Cook looked askance at the unusual situation since the young woman rarely took an interest in food preparation at all. She got up from the stool and went to the cabinet where the percolator had been stowed after breakfast and took it out.

"Ah," Amanda said, as if she knew it was there all along before looking around for where the coffee grounds might be.

"Let me do it, Miss," Cook said, taking it to the deep stone sink and filling the pot with water. "I'll bring it out to you when it's done."

"Know your way around the kitchen, eh?" Brendan teased as they went back to the sitting room. Amanda pretended not to hear the remark. Mr. Burnside met them as he came out of the library.

"Daddy. I thought you'd be at the office by now."

"Hello, Mr. Halloran," he said, and the men shook hands.

"I might ask the same of you," her father said.

"I went to see Kitty. And I won't be going in at all today."

"Terrible business," Mr. Burnside said. "I meant to leave for work a long time ago, but several impatient clients have been pestering my secretary about some things, and she has been calling and relaying messages. It's pointless since I can't do anything while I'm here."

"What's it about?"

He looked at them both, gauging how much to say. "It's about the matter I mentioned at breakfast. It looks like we've lost an employee."

Amanda gasped.

"No, he's very much alive. Just not here in Boston. Had to go to Denver for his health. It was sudden. You know, it's usual in the business world to give at least two weeks' notice," Mr. Burnside said pointedly to Amanda.

"Yes, I do know that. You don't imagine I'm going to suddenly quit because Mr. Barlow is going to leave?"

"I hope not. One's reputation must always be protected."

"And I'm assuming Mr. Barlow is not going for at least another two weeks. Perhaps longer. The hospital board will need to find a new Director and that could take some time."

Mr. Burnside went to gather his briefcase from the study and, when he returned, said to Amanda, "If you're not going to the hospital today, why don't you come in with me? See if you can make some sense out of Gilbert's files. My secretary said they are a bit of a mess."

"Me?"

"Yes, you pride yourself on organization. You like to sort things out, aren't I right?" Mr. Burnside said to Brendan.

Brendan was shifting from foot to foot during the discussion and finally said, "Speaking of which, I ought to be going into work myself."

"What about the coffee?" Amanda asked.

"Another time, thank you."

"Yes, sorry to hold you up," Mr. Burnside said, and he let his daughter lead the man to the front door.

"What sort of work did the employee do who left so suddenly?" Brendan asked.

"He was a private investigator," Amanda said with a smile.

"Uh-oh," he groaned in response, running his fingers through his hair. "Don't get into trouble."

"I never do. It's just that trouble seems to find me." Amanda turned to make sure her father was not watching them and gave Brendan a kiss goodbye before gently pushing him out the door.

Chapter 3

Before Mr. Burnside and Amanda could leave, they had to wait for Louisa, who needed a ride to Monsieur Josef's salon, and it was a long delay.

"What in the world is that girl doing?" he asked.

"Beauty takes time," Amanda said.

"She's beautiful enough as it is. That's the whole problem."

Louisa came down the stairs carefully with a large portfolio tucked under her arm. She could see the annoyance on her father's face.

"Well, if you would buy me a car, you wouldn't have to chauffeur me everywhere," she said.

"You seem to get where you need to be without my help at other times," he replied, referring to her ability to go to Rob Worley's nightclub in the evenings more times than he knew about. "And are you wearing makeup?"

"Oh, Daddy, really. Everyone does. Look at Amanda. Powder, rouge, eyebrow pencil, mascara and lipstick. All very tastefully applied."

He looked at his older daughter. "I never realized. All your mother wears is powder and lipstick."

"I know," Louisa said. "Still, about that car…."

"You and your sister can share."

"Just a minute," Amanda began. "If you recall, I paid half of the purchase price. If Louisa would like to reimburse me for half of my half, I might consider it." She knew that Louisa was not a saver, and it was not a likely scenario.

Her sister stamped her foot. "You'll come into your trust money soon and you could at least show some generosity to me for all I've done for you."

"And what might that be?"

"Lending you my evening gowns, for one thing."

"That's lending, not half ownership."

"That's enough, girls. With the economy as it has been lately, I don't know what we can expect from your grandparents' gift that constitutes the trust. Frankly, with everything else going on in the world, my work and this family, I haven't paid it much attention lately. But I will look into it shortly. In the meantime, can we please get going?" He jammed his hat on his head, and Louisa laughed at his grouchy expression and kissed him on the cheek.

"Okay, Mr. Grumpypants. Let's get this show on the road."

They filed down to the garage on the lower level at the back of the house and Louisa maneuvered the portfolio into the back seat beside her.

"What the devil is that?"

"Sketches for some gowns. I told you all about it the other day."

He grumbled in return.

"Is Monsieur Josef going to pay you or are you an apprentice?" Amanda asked.

"We haven't sorted that out, yet. But I hope to impress him with these designs and then do some bargaining. He might want me to model in the salon, too."

Mr. Burnside glowered into the rearview mirror at her.

"Daddy, it's all on the up and up. His usual customers come in —all women, by the way—and the models show them how the dresses look on a living person, not a hanger. It's important for them to see the clothes in motion and feel the fabric. They always buy something."

"Who is that man, anyway? Your mother doesn't shop with him, does she?"

"No, I'm afraid not. But I might point her in that direction. His clientele is made up of established young matrons with exquisite taste. They're very chic."

They continued in silence until reaching the salon, located in Boston's tony shopping district already bustling with women, some arm in arm enjoying a day out.

"Bye, now!" Louisa said with a wave.

"I don't think I understand half of what she just said," Mr. Burnside said. "It's a good thing you have a head on your shoulders."

"Let's put it to good use today because I will have to show my face at the hospital tomorrow."

"Don't worry. I'm sure my secretary exaggerated about the tumult."

Whether she had made more of the situation than was reasonable made no difference; Miss Brunson was visibly agitated when Mr. Burnside introduced Amanda.

"I'm so glad you're going to help. There have been several clients calling this morning and asking for updates," Miss Brunson said, shuffling through paper squares for the appropriate messages. She bent her head and Amanda could see the precision with which she had arranged her hair, similar to the organization of her work area. She handed the stack to Mr. Burnside, who walked into his office with his daughter and closed the door.

"She tends to be excitable," he whispered although the secretary could not possibly have overheard behind the heavy wooden door.

"Where shall I begin, Mr. Burnside?" Amanda asked.

He looked at her in surprise. "Are you going to call me that?"

"Of course. I can't very well call you Daddy in this professional environment."

"All right, Miss Burnside. Let me put down my briefcase and I'll show you Gilbert's office."

"Is Gilbert his first name or surname?"

"Last. William Gilbert. I don't know why we refer to him by his surname. All right, let's go then."

Miss Brunson was fingering her necklace as they passed her desk and Amanda wondered why she was so concerned about the man who had abruptly left his employment. It became obvious when Mr. Burnside pushed open the door to his office and saw the state of things. If there had been papers on the desk at one time, they were now entirely on the floor, scattered among the folders in which they may have originally been. He groaned and shook his head.

"Is this how he kept his office or has someone else been in here?" Amanda asked, stooping to pick up an empty file folder to read the label.

Mr. Burnside stepped over the papers as best he could to retrieve a metal object that he put on the desk. "This was his file organizer and evidently someone has been in here."

"Don't worry. I'll pick these up and see if I can sort them into some kind of order. I assume these are organized by client name?"

"Yes. He was also in the habit of putting the first initial on any piece of paper he added to the file along with the date it was written. He was methodical that way."

"It shouldn't be all that difficult to reassemble them. Can you tell me who these clients are?"

"The name is on each folder. But one is a delicate domestic issue, if you get my drift, so please don't go reading the actual notes if you can help it. There's also a case about the provenance of a painting and several instances of tracing the financial dealings of business partners who had fallen out. Dry stuff. Do you need anything else?" he asked.

"Yes. How about I poke my head out about one o'clock and you can take me to lunch?"

Mr. Burnside smiled. "Absolutely. At my club. Remember, don't do too much reading. Just sorting."

She saluted her father as he closed the door behind him. No reading? That was impossible. It took her some time to just get the papers right side up and amassed into a pile, then with the five folders in front of her, she sorted the papers according to the initials corresponding to the cases. Then it was only a matter of putting each folder's worth into chronological order. It was tedious and some sheets of paper had no more than a few written lines while others were single-spaced typed observations, making it seem as if he were tracking the information for the purposes of the law firm's billing system. In among the papers was a tally sheet neatly logging how many hours he had devoted to each case and the last entry was three days prior.

Amanda looked at her watch. It was only eleven-thirty and, while she had looked at the contents of the financial dispute cases, they were mostly bank statements, handwritten invoices and receipts in an assortment of styles and what must have been Mr. Gilbert's notes from various telephone conversations or in-person meetings that were dated and the time noted. Boring stuff as far as she was concerned.

Now, for the domestic case, which was labeled only with initials, she read what seemed to be a husband being unfaithful to his wife and the investigator following the man's activities over a period of weeks. Work, lunches with male colleagues, work, home and then attendance at a play with his wife. Several days of this which made Amanda wonder why the wife had her suspicions since he seemed to be home with her or out with her every evening. Four days later, the husband was followed to a hotel on the outskirts of town during the lunch hour where he checked in and out within the space of an hour and half. No lunch that day. Amanda looked at the date—three weeks prior. So, Gilbert continued his meticulous surveillance and a pattern had formed where once a week the husband would check into a different hotel at the lunch hour, presumably not having room service. But there was no mention of whom he was seeing. Perhaps Gilbert didn't stick around long enough to witness the partner in these deceptions. As she read the next sheet the investigator had inadvertently used the man's surname and Amanda's eyes popped wide.

"I can't believe it!" she said. It was the father of one of her debutante friends. She closed the file abruptly. He seemed a perfectly normal father-like person, not someone sneaking around with who-knows-who in random hotel rooms. She grimaced in disgust and decided not to think about this case any further. And she would most definitely not tell her father she had read the files.

The last folder was the provenance case and there were letters back and forth from someone to a Mr. Scofield, a gallery owner and art dealer whose name she recognized, regarding the authenticity of a particular painting. Strangely, the piece of art in question belonged to the Warren family, which piqued her interest. It seemed that the investigator's work for this case consisted of collecting paperwork rather than following people around clandestinely to seedy locations. If this was what private investigation consisted of, she wouldn't mind it at all. Creeping around to see if spouses were cheating on each other was another matter. Much too distasteful. As she flipped through the pages, one of them was a photograph of a familiar looking painting with a woman seated in front of it in old-fashioned clothes. The woman's pose reminded her of the painting of Whistler's Mother that her parents had taken her to see when on loan to the Museum of Fine Arts. In both the painting and the photograph, the subject was seated facing left although this woman wore something more like an evening dress in an exotic pattern, not the austere costume that James McNeill Whistler's mother wore for his iconic painting.

A knock on the door startled Amanda and she saw her father smiling at her.

"All done?"

"Yes, it wasn't such a difficult job after all. I was just looking at this photograph and it seems an interesting case."

Mr. Burnside approached and looked over her shoulder. "Yes, not my client, but I heard about it in a partner's meeting. Well, then, off to lunch!" he said.

Amanda got out of the chair and caught her foot on the edge of the desk and stumbled. "So clumsy of me," she said. But as she regained her balance, she saw another piece of paper under the desk that she had previously overlooked. She opened it, read it swiftly and gave it to her father.

It read: "Stop immediately. Your life depends on it."

He said, "I can't imagine who sent this to Gilbert—if it was intended for him—but it could explain his recent sudden illness."

Chapter 4

Louisa had walked confidently into the double door entrance of Monsieur Josef's salon and inhaled the faint scent of some woman's perfume. Another private client had evidently made an appointment and, judging by his closed office door, they were discussing her requirements and preferences. Off to the right up a set of stairs was the atelier where the clothes were constructed by a group of four small women who had worked together for years and had no need of chatter. Several mannequins were arranged around the bright room and one of the women was on tiptoe draping an already basted garment onto a form. Louisa said hello to the group, and they all nodded and muttered, "Mademoiselle."

She was sure that none of them were from France or spoke French, but it seemed to be the custom in these types of salons that everyone was either Madame, Monsieur or Mademoiselle. Despite the owner's lofty name and slight accent, Louisa had the suspicion that he was as American as she, but the Continental allusion was perfect for this business. She took her large portfolio case over to a table under the windows, took off her coat, unzipped the canvas, took out the tablet, and pulled back the cover to reveal a sketch for an evening gown. Greta took her glasses off and put down her needle to come over and look.

"That's very nice. He will like it. Especially the flow of the skirt. Chiffon?"

"I had that in mind. Wouldn't it be lovely in a Nile green?" Louisa asked.

Greta nodded approval and went back to her task.

In the side compartment of the portfolio case was a set of pastel crayons and Louisa took out green, blue and yellow and drew out lines of color on a blank portion at the bottom of the drawing, blending them with her finger. She was pleased with the result and tore the sheet of paper carefully from the tablet. Underneath was a sketch for a spring suit—even though it was winter—because she had quickly picked up the notion of working at least one season ahead. The costume was fitted at the waist with a peplum over a straight skirt and all she could think of was robin's egg blue. Perfect for Easter.

Footsteps on the stairs caught her attention as Jeanne, Monsieur's assistant, came into the room dressed in black, as usual.

"Mademoiselle, he wishes to see you." She turned and Louisa followed her down the curved staircase, not to his office but to an adjacent lounge where he sat across from a young woman who was already familiar to her.

"May I present Señora Guzmán." Louisa held out her hand and tilted her head to one side and smiled.

"We're already acquainted," Louisa said since Caroline was a regular at Rob's club, which was financed by her husband, José.

The petite blonde laughed. "Yes. What a ridiculously small town Boston is. Please, sit down." Caroline took a cigarette from a gold case and Monsieur Josef produced a lighter. After she had taken her first inhalation, she continued. "Her sister Amanda is the girl who broke my brother's heart." It was a stinging comment, although she said it lightly.

"Surely not! I saw Valerie's engagement notice in the newspaper. He must have a fantastic constitution to have had his heart heal so quickly."

"Well, he is a doctor."

"So, you ladies know each other. Splendid. Señora Guzmán is looking to order some bespoke garments for upcoming events connected with the gallery, is that correct?"

"That's right, I'd forgotten you owned a gallery."

"That was in Manhattan. The Crash took care of that quickly. Now I'm working for Scofield as things are picking up. He's awfully modern, as is the art he exhibits and represents. That's why he's not Mister Scofield.

Louisa hadn't given a thought to the art market downturn nor was she aware that things were improving.

"I'm in need of what you could call cocktail dresses—not gowns—for hosting evening showings at the gallery." She blew a stream of smoke to the side and turned her smile on Louisa.

"Tea length and elegant but not too much decolletage?"

"Exactly. I don't want to be too distracting to potential buyers or have their wives think I have something else in mind. It must speak of quiet wealth and impeccable taste. But artsy."

"We have some things like that we could show you," Monsieur Josef said, standing. "Let me get one of the models if you'll step into the showroom. If nothing suits, perhaps Louisa could sketch something for you."

Minutes later Jeanne had already provided Caroline with tea, Monsieur Josef had instructed the only model working that day to get ready, meaning out of her robe, while he went through the racks and selected three dresses that came close to the description the client had given him.

"I'll get Jeanne to help," he said, meaning to zip her up and find any accessories that might add to the look.

Louisa had gone up to the atelier to retrieve her sketching tablet and a pencil and was back down in the salon before the model came in wearing the first outfit. It was a subdued floor length dress with a matching evening jacket and the model walked down to where the women sat, Monsieur Josef standing behind, and removed the jacket showing a modest neckline and cap sleeves.

"Almost. But that's more like something to wear to the opera. And the length is wrong."

The boss waved his hand at the model, who walked back to the dressing room to change into the next outfit. Meanwhile, Louisa was busy drawing and only looked up later when the model came back in a different look. This dress was brighter in color and by the expression on Caroline's face, it wasn't what she had in mind.

"That's more like a garden party frock," she said.

"What do you think of this idea?" Louisa said, looking up at Monsieur Josef first for approval and then showing her sketch to Caroline. "I'm guessing that one ought to project a modern look. If you're showing modern art, you can't look sedate or conservative."

"Exactly. Although Scofield deals in antiquities and represen-tational art, the big thing now is the splashy, showy pieces." She looked at Louisa's drawing. "Yes, that's the mood. A bit unconventional but it must be black. It's just what's expected."

"A bit of a drop waist on one side?" Monsieur Josef suggested. "To add some angularity."

"Yes. With such a modern dress, I may have to get some inno-vative hairstyle."

Louisa and her boss looked at Caroline and they both shook their heads as she laughed at their reaction.

"I don't suppose I could pull off some dramatic thing like having my hair pulled back into a severe chignon. This mop will have to do."

Hardly a mop, Louisa thought. It looked as if she had just come from the hairdresser.

"Well, then, let us get going on some mock-ups and we can have you back in a few days for a fitting. We have your measurements upstairs for reference."

After Caroline left, Louisa asked if she could use the salon's telephone.

"Of course," Jeanne said. "Just be sure that you don't make a long-distance call or stay on the line a long time. Business comes first. And remember, there are other extensions in the building so your call might not be private."

"Never mind that. I just have to check in with a friend about transportation." Louisa went into the model's changing area, nodded to the girl, and then looked at the phone. The girl took a cigarette case and a lighter from her purse and went out a door that led to the fire escape.

"Rob, hello. I've finally got a chance to call you."

"I'm glad you caught me. Things are moving quickly, and I've got to keep pace with the news."

"What's that?"

"The states voting on the 21st Amendment."

"Oh, that."

"Yes, that. Repeal of Prohibition. We're getting closer to the three-quarters vote needed to make alcohol legal."

"But I thought you were already allowed to sell wine and three-two beer?" Louisa was only half listening to Rob since she sensed that someone was outside in the hallway.

"We've got to replace all that inventory with the real thing once the ban is lifted. No one is going to want to drink the low-point stuff after that. And we're in a race against every other establishment in Boston—and the state for that matter —to secure contracts with the Canadian producers."

"So, you're very busy. So am I. I just got a commission to design some clothing for none other than Caroline Guzmán. I think my career is beginning with a bang." At that point Louisa heard a click and said, "I think someone else here wants to use the phone, so I'll call you later from home." She hung up and quickly reviewed if there had been anything said in her side of the conversation that was not appropriate. As far as what Rob had talked about, it was an open secret that there were nightclubs where people had been buying alcohol since Prohibition began. With the relaxing of the restrictions, there was even less concern knowing the advent of total repeal was on its way and the police would have bigger fish to fry.

Louisa weighed whether to take a taxi home since she had to lug the portfolio case with her and then decided to call her father whose office was close. Miss Brunson answered and told her that Mr. Burnside and Amanda were about to leave for his club for lunch. On an impulse, she said she would join them shortly and hung up before there could be any dispute. Why did Amanda get all the special treatment?

Louisa breezed into the club's dining room and waved to her father and sister and came up to their table that had already been set for three.

"Miss Brunson gave me a heads up," he said with a smile.

"I was hoping to surprise you," she said, planting a kiss on his cheek.

"Everything you do surprises me."

"How was the drudgery of the law offices, Amanda?"

"Actually interesting. I'm just sorting through papers and folders trying to put things in order. I'm afraid I don't have the head for the intricacies of legal issues."

"Don't sell yourself short," her father said. "You have an excellent mind. But to be a lawyer there is some expectation that you have a college degree. And then you must 'read' with a practicing attorney although law school is becoming the more preferred option. It depends, of course. If you know you are interested in criminal law, for example, suffering through torts and contracts may seem a waste of time. Although as far as I am concerned, any bit of knowledge gleaned is not a waste of time."

"As if any law school would take a woman," Louisa added, taking a bread stick from the basket.

"They have for some time. Not too many. And I'm sorry to say that many firms are not interested in hiring women."

"That's settled, then," Amanda said. "I do like a challenge, but I'm not going to hit my head against a brick wall just to say I did it."

The waiter brought three glasses of sherry to the table and went to Mr. Burnside, who put in the order for himself and his two daughters.

"And what have you been up to today?" he asked Louisa.

"Very exciting. I had some sketches to show Monsieur Josef although he left the building before I could show him the entire portfolio. But he had a client—you'll never guess who— Caroline Browne. She now styles herself as Señora Guzmán. More exotic, I suppose."

"That's interesting. It seems she veers between spending money and thinking she doesn't have enough. They're still living with her mother," Amanda said.

"It's hardly like they're crammed into a third-floor, cold water walk-up. The Brownes' home is large enough to even accommodate Fred. I wonder if Valerie is going to move in with them after they get married?" Louisa glanced at her sister for a reaction, but none was forthcoming.

"Good luck to them all if that is the case," Mr. Burnside said with a chuckle. He had never been fond of Amanda's dour former suitor.

"Remember Caroline used to have an art gallery in Manhattan? She said she had to give it up. I suppose that market may have improved because she's working for Scofield Gallery You know, all that modern art."

Amanda and her father looked at each other for a moment recognizing the name.

"And I guess she shows people around and she needed what you could only call artsy outfits."

"What on earth does that mean?" her father asked.

"She can't be selling these large pieces of incomprehensible abstract art wearing a gingham dress and apron."

Amanda laughed. "As if Caroline has ever had either one!"

"Figuratively speaking, of course. She wants to make a splash and she said that Scofield is very successful. So at least I'm getting somewhere."

If Scofield was doing so well, it stood to reason that his reputation was important. He likely was well connected to people who could verify the authenticity of older works, but perhaps he was more interested in the motivations of the seller. She had already flagged that case as something she ought to pay close attention to since it involved her friend Kitty's family. Amanda smiled at her sister's enthusiasm and decided she would spend the afternoon looking more closely at that particular folder.

Chapter 5

After the heavy lunch, Amanda struggled to keep awake, but being incorrigibly curious plowed on reading Gilbert's files. She decided to jot down names mentioned in the folders for follow-up questions; the most obvious place to begin was the attorneys who had authorized the cases in the first place. Not to overstep her authority—if any had been given to her—she asked her father if it was appropriate to talk to those men to get some background. He thought it was a good idea and called each of them for her and arranged it, letting her know that if there were issues of client confidentiality, the lawyer would be sure to let her know.

"Relating to this alleged infidelity case Gilbert was working on, I think I ought to give back the file to the attorney as it is. If he wishes to have it pursued, there must be someone else who could do the legwork," she said.

"Of course, I had no intention of you actually doing any of the investigating on that subject!"

"Don't sound so horrified. After all, I have done my fair share of sleuthing," she said.

"And I understood it all happened by accident. The notion of you pursuing such a thing as a hobby is, well, not suitable."

The fact that her father was so adamant about her not pursuing it only strengthened her resolve that it *was* perfectly suitable. And perhaps not as a hobby. But that was all wrapped up in whether her position in the hospital would continue without Mr. Barlow or if she wanted to move to Hartford to continue working for him. The best course of action was to put all those decisions out of her mind for the moment. So, she just smiled at her father without responding.

"Sometimes I think you are more dangerous when you don't say anything and just smile," he commented.

AMANDA MET FIRST with Mr. Carson, one of the partners, and he thanked her for volunteering to help.

"What I've found is that your name was associated with two folders, each concerning a disagreement between former business associates." She handed them over and he put his reading glasses on and opened the first.

"Ah, yes, Gilbert had tracked down quite a few documents. He turned through the pages and shook his head from side to side. "I'll need to look at these more closely to see if he managed to dig anything up that was helpful. And the second?" He held out his hand for the folder that Amanda extended to him. "This case! You might not believe it, but these two individuals have been bickering about this issue for several years. There's almost an entire file drawer full of paperwork."

"That's a shame."

"The funny thing is that they still work together, and their company is successful. I think that if they would put as much energy into expanding their business as they have in nitpicking the division of earnings, they'd be on top of the world." He let out a laugh. "But such is human nature. Do you want these back?"

"I thought I should give them to you to look over and see if Mr. Gilbert had completed his investigation. If not, these could go back into his office for when he returns." Although she didn't say it, she wondered if he was going to return.

"I'm afraid that is not any time soon. Chest issues," he said, patting his own.

Her father had said asthma but maybe he thought it was tuberculosis. She didn't know and wasn't going to ask for clarification.

"Perhaps the firm will engage someone else to follow up."

"We may have to. And thank you again."

"You're quite welcome," she responded as he stood to shake her hand.

The domestic case belonged to Mr. Van Eaton, and Amanda wondered if it was because of his junior position that they gave him a less desirable case where the more established members might know the couple involved. She tapped on the slightly open door, and he welcomed her in. He was not a partner and appeared to be quite new to the firm; glancing at the date of the diploma on the wall, her suspicions were confirmed.

"I was putting some of Mr. Gilbert's files in order and saw that this was your case that he was assisting with."

"Please, sit down," he said, standing up while she did so and taking the folder from her. Upon opening it up, his face flushed, and he quickly asked, "Did you read through this?"

"My task was to put the papers in chronological order since they were scattered all over the floor when we opened his office."

"That's quite unlike Gilbert," Mr. Van Eaton said. "Are you the new secretary?"

"No, I'm Amanda Burnside. My father asked me to come in to help sort through things. Just for the day."

"Oh, your father...." His face became redder, and he turned away and flicked through the papers until his embarrassment subsided. When he turned back, they looked at one another and he was about to say something when she interrupted him.

"I know it must be a sensitive situation, so I was careful to avert my eyes to much of the narration." This, of course, was nonsense. How could she not read the entire file once she recognized the surname? To think that her friend's father was traipsing around Boston, in and out of various hotels on the outskirts to meet with some woman, was shocking. Even more startling was that his wife had somehow caught wind of the affair and had hired her father's firm to represent her to secure enough evidence. Divorce was not common among the Boston Brahmin since they valued their respectability too highly and did not want to be seen as 'common.' It was also a gamble for a soon-to-be ex-wife since she would get alimony, the house, and a further settlement, but could not retain the same standard of living. In addition, her social standing would be ruined despite the situation not being her fault. Single young women had a place in society as did spinsters and widows, but the term divorcée had a tinge of the naughty about it. Just the previous year there had been a Broadway musical called *The Gay Divorcée*, but the notion that a divorced woman was light-hearted and free to seek her pursuits was a thing of fiction in Boston society. The only women Amanda knew who were divorced were shunned: a lonely tradeoff for initiating the action.

"I'll leave the file with you," Amanda said, having read as much as she could stomach.

Mr. Van Eaton seemed greatly relieved.

The remaining folder was the investigation into the provenance of a painting, and the interesting part was that it was Mr. Scofield, the man at whose gallery Caroline Guzmán now worked, who had initiated the matter. Well, Boston was a small town. Amanda had skimmed through the papers previously and, reading them more thoroughly, found that the painting in question was jointly owned by brothers Rupert and August Warren. She wondered if it was usual for a gallery owner, hired to sell artwork at a commission, to be concerned about the financial standing of the owners. It would seem obvious that they were selling because they needed the funds. When she sought out the attorney who had originated the matter, she found he was not in that day. Rather than give it to his secretary or leave it on his desk, she brought it back to Gilbert's office, where she did not put it into his metal file organizer but set it aside for further perusal.

Amanda felt pleased with herself that she had accomplished so much in just one-half day and decided to poke around in the drawers of the desk. In the top drawer were the usual desk accoutrements: a stapler, pencils, scissors and a ruler. Reaching back further, she pulled out a certificate indicating that he was a licensed private investigator. And she wondered how one went about getting such a license and if it were necessary in order to do that kind of work. By the looks of Gilbert's work product, it was observational and notational in nature. It wasn't like the silly movies that depicted people racing around with guns and gangsters shooting at one another in dark alleys.

The side drawer had a ball made of rubber bands, paper clips and bottles of ink. The larger drawer below was stuffed to the top with more sheets of paper. Amanda groaned. No wonder the job of sorting seemed so easy. It was because she hadn't even begun to skim the surface of what he had done. To her dismay, these were more documents relating to the Scofield file as well as some cryptic notes that were neither dated nor had an initial associated with it. Was this part of the firm's business or something else? And of all the files she had looked at, which one did she think warranted a threatening note?

It was only three o'clock, so Amanda took out the mess of papers and began trying to make sense of them. Those that were connected to a case she put into separate groups, leaving the mystery notes in front of her. She was puzzling over one that she had read and to whom it referred when her father knocked on the door jamb, his coat over his arm and hat in hand.

"You seem mesmerized. Interesting reading?"

"More confusing than anything. Oh, time to go?"

"Unless you want to burn the midnight oil."

"No, I've had enough for the day. Brendan and I are going to dinner tonight and I'm meeting with Kitty tomorrow as well as Mr. Barlow."

"Busy girl," her father said, taking her coat from the rack in the corner and helping her into it.

"Lots of decisions to make."

As they drove home, he asked her what she made of the work she had done that day.

"It was tedious trying to put things back together. Do you think Mr. Gilbert purposefully made a mess of the paperwork? Who else could have gone into his office?"

"I can't imagine. We all have desks with locks since we often deal with sensitive issues."

"It looks like he didn't lock his desk," Amanda said. "It's almost as if he left in a hurry."

They had stopped at an intersection where a police officer directed traffic and Mr. Burnside looked at his daughter.

"Do you think his rapid departure was not necessarily health-related?"

A whistle blew and Mr. Burnside turned his attention back to the road where the traffic policeman waved him forward with a white-gloved hand and a scowl.

"What do you think?" Amanda asked knowing her father had no answer.

They came home to the sight of Mrs. Burnside and Louisa in the sitting room, the young woman excitedly telling of her conquest of the fashion world to her mother's delight.

"And to think that you've never designed anything for me," Amanda accused her lightheartedly.

"I've only just begun my illustrious career," Louisa answered.

"That's so like you. You just dipped your toe into the water and you're already swimming across the English Channel," Amanda said.

Louisa smiled at what she perceived had been a compliment. Amanda retreated to her room to freshen up before her dinner date but couldn't get out of her mind the crossroads at which she stood. What now? Talk to Mrs. Tyrell, the Mercy Hospital Board Chair, to let her stay on doing her current job? What if the new director wasn't interested in expanding the remote clinics? What about the possibility of going to Hartford? It was only about one hundred miles away and she could come home each weekend. And what would her job be? Another thought occurred to her: Mr. Barlow had not been at his current job that long. Was his energy dependent upon facing new challenges in new locations, meaning he might change jobs again soon and then what? The questions rolled around in her brain and all she wanted to do was have a moment's peace.

A splash of cold water on her face, reapplication of her minimal makeup and combing her hair did the trick. Although she knew she and Brendan would discuss this at dinner, for now she pushed the thoughts from her mind and forced a smile at herself in the mirror.

"WHERE ARE you taking me for dinner tonight?" Amanda asked as they cruised along Commonwealth Avenue.

"I thought we should try a Chinese place recommended to me," he said.

"Aye, aye, Captain," she responded.

"Slight correction," he said with a smile. "As of this morning it's Lieutenant."

"What?" She turned to him and caught him beaming. "It's official?"

"Yes. And at long last. I may have Dominick to thank for the promotion since he had the other detectives pestering the

Chief to make a decision about a permanent supervisor for the division."

"That's wonderful." She leaned over and kissed him on the cheek.

"Careful—you'll distract my driving."

"You didn't have to pass any grueling qualifying exam or interrogations by some board? Walk on hot coals?"

"Nope. The Chief has the authority to make those appointments. Which means he can also un-appoint me if dissatisfied."

"That hardly seems fair."

"Don't worry, I'll hold my own. Although there are rumblings about these things from time to time. Officers wanting to have a competitive process as you suggested rather than serving at the pleasure of the Chief. It would be more fair but in this case, I'm not complaining."

"It seems to me that he dragged his feet long enough, having you do the work without the title."

"Or the pay raise. But that has been resolved, too." He patted her arm.

Amanda couldn't imagine why she had never had a meal in a Chinese restaurant but then thought that it was in what her mother would term a rougher area of town. But looking around, she didn't sense any danger or menacing people. The past year working at the hospital and going out with Brendan had exposed her to many parts of the city that were new to her, an eye-opening experience that made her a little sorry for the limitations people put on their experiences when there was so much to see.

They were greeted at the door by a woman with a square-cut short jacket and black pants who ushered them to the only unoccupied booth. Although the space was full, the diners were eating quietly. The entire place was decorated in red with gold accents and images of dragons and clouds.

The woman gave them menus and returned almost immediately with a pot of tea and two small cups.

"It smells like jasmine, or am I imagining that?"

"It could be. No milk and sugar now."

"There are so many selections on this menu—how can I possibly decide if I don't even know what these are? I certainly don't want to seem like a tourist and order chow mein or chop suey, both of which I've had and thought were tasteless."

"The key to their cuisine is mixing different ingredients with various preparations. So, braising or stir-frying or breading and frying. You get the picture. It's an ingenious way of creating something new from familiar items."

"I'm afraid you'll have to guide me." She put the menu down. "Better yet, why don't you order for me? You've come to know my taste. I'll try just about anything as long as it's not eyeballs."

"Anything?" He teased raising one dark eyebrow.

"Something with pork would be nice," she said.

"All right, how about twice-cooked pork with snow peas and water chestnuts."

"Sounds delightful. I don't think I've had water chestnuts before. Or snow peas."

"Light and crunchy. I think you'll like it."

A young man came from the kitchen and brought a trolley, delivering two covered dishes and two bowls of rice to a nearby table before coming to where they sat and asking what they wanted. Brendan ordered and when the man left, he explained that this restaurant, like many others in the city, were family run.

"Mother is behind the cash register and seats the guests. Sons and daughters wait on the tables and father is the chef. All in the family. It makes for long days, but these folks are eager to make a good life for themselves, better than what they had in China. You wait, in one generation these folks will own banks."

Amanda sipped her tea.

"Speaking of making a life, what have you decided about Mr. Barlow's offer?" he asked.

She hadn't expected him to come to the point so soon, but now that it was out in the open, she knew she had to face the question.

"First, I don't know what job he is offering exactly. Secretary? No, thank you. Aside from the fact that I don't know how to type and shorthand would be beyond me, that would be a dull thing to relocate for."

"I'm sure he has nothing like that in mind. He probably would like you to be his assistant. If not more."

"What does that mean?" she asked.

"He thinks highly of your skills. Why, do you think he has romantic notions as well?"

"Brendan, how can you think that?"

"He's not married, is he?"

41

Amanda paused before answering. "No, but he hasn't ever made any advances. None at all."

"Hmm," was his response.

"Hartford is a bit more than an hour's drive. I could work there during the week and come home on the weekends."

"Is that what you want to do?"

"I'm not sure what I want to do."

"Well, then let me be clear about what I would like you to do. I would like very much for you to stay here in Boston."

"Is that a demand?"

"No. A request. A wish. In more romantic terms, I think you could consider it a declaration of love and my intentions for the future."

"Oh," was all she could muster.

They sipped their tea for a few minutes while thoughts raced through both their minds.

For Brendan: was that too forward? Too oblique? Too soon?

For Amanda: he's made his position clear. Now what?

Their ruminations were cut short by the arrival of the food, two covered dishes and two bowls of rice along with chopsticks and forks. They busied themselves taking off the lids and inspecting the food.

"Amanda, on second thought, I know you are an independent woman, and you want to achieve something with your life. But I want to let you know that I have come to love you and if you feel the same, then your going to Hartford or anywhere else out of my sight would be devastating."

She burst into tears, catching the attention of some of the other diners whom she waved away, letting them know everything was all right. It was more than all right. She had yet to talk to Mr. Barlow, but she knew what her answer would be, and her heart soared.

Chapter 6

It was with some trepidation that Amanda went to Mercy Hospital the next day to talk to Mr. Barlow. His office door was closed and, at first, she thought that he hadn't yet arrived, but after asking Miss Bailey she got the shocking answer.

"He's sorting and packing," she said with red-rimmed eyes.

"Don't worry, I'm sure your job is safe."

"It's not that. It's that he was the nicest boss I've ever had."

Amanda nodded with a sigh. "I'd have to agree. I know he wanted to talk to me—do you think this is a good time?"

Miss Bailey reached for the intercom button, but Amanda held out a hand to stop her.

"Let me take off my coat and hat at least," she said, walking down the hall to the little room that was her office. It made her sad to think that she might be leaving the dingy place where she had spent so many hours working on the outreach projects. There were two small desks, hers piled with papers and notes, the other where Valerie had briefly worked until her engagement to Fred had been announced. Now, everything was about the other young woman's spring wedding, and she had no time to volunteer at the hospital.

Taking a few deep breaths to calm herself, Amanda went back to the front desk and gave Miss Bailey a nod. The announcement was made, and Mr. Barlow opened the door with a broad smile.

"There you are! I was sorry to hear about your friend's loss. That must have been difficult. She is lucky to have your support."

Amanda walked into the chaos of boxes and papers laid out on the desk and the adjacent worktable.

"Welcome to my going-away party," he said cheerfully. He moved folders off the chair that faced his desk so she could sit down. "Let's have a chat."

"Mr. Barlow, I didn't know that you had been looking for another job. It came as a complete shock to me."

He gave a chuckle. "One thing you learn as you climb the ladder, as you surely will, is to recognize the signs that you're not being effective anymore."

"What do you mean? Look at all that you've done. The man who sat in that chair before you couldn't hold a candle to your achievements. The renovation, the expansion of the outreach clinics—that's a lot."

"That's what you saw because you were a part of it. But the Board's attitude toward me had been cooling." He picked up a pen and fiddled with it.

"Mrs. Tyrell was so excited to hire you. She'd never let you go."

"Ah, that's where you missed something. She's the Board Chair for a reason. They elected her to keep her busy with the minutiae of the meetings, the committees and the fundraising while the others hold the power behind her back. She's only one vote, after all."

"You can't be serious. Has anyone spoken to you indicating that they don't want you here anymore?"

"Of course not. It's the small slights, the impromptu meetings that take place without inviting me. Oh, I know the Board is the decision-making body, but if they thought my input was of value, they would have included me more. They let me go my merry way, getting involved with the community, which isn't as important to them. More fool I, not to have seen the signs sooner. So, I put out my feelers, looking for another position, to have the dignity of resigning rather than being shown the door. Hence, the Hartford job."

"What is it?"

"Director of the hospital there. Oddly, it is larger than Mercy because there is no competition from other institutions and the city takes a keen interest and supplies some of the funding. It's a plum job. That's why I thought you might like to come along and ride on my coattails."

"What sort of job did you have in mind for me?"

Barlow held the pen up by the ends and turned it over as if reading something written on it. He put it down suddenly and looked up at her.

"I would like you to be my Executive Assistant."

Amanda paused. "What would that entail?"

He laughed. "Whatever I need you to do! I heard you were the person to organize the debutante ball in your year, you've dealt here with some pretty tough neighborhood big shots, the police, and you know the monied folks in town. I feel sure you could do the same in a new community."

Amanda looked down at her lap and was struggling to form an answer.

"Ah, I sense a hesitation," he said.

"I've spent my whole life in Boston. My family is here. My friends are here."

"And I'm guessing there is some romantic interest as well."

"Yes," she said, feeling herself blush.

"Serious?"

"Yes, I think so. But even if that weren't the case, I don't feel ready to leave yet."

"Understood." Mr. Barlow stood up and came around to her side of the desk as she stood as well. He put out his hand and shook hers. "It has been wonderful working with you."

She shook his hand and quickly left.

"You're not leaving, too, are you?" Miss Bailey said to her retreating figure.

"Not yet. I think. I don't know," Amanda said, fighting back tears. When she got back to her office, she let them flow freely, admonishing herself for being so emotional. She was startled when the telephone rang; she picked it up.

"Amanda, it's me, Kitty. Can you come over and help me with some things?" She sounded painfully lost.

"Right away." Selfishly, she thought it would be good to get away from the hospital before anyone got wind of what was happening.

The Warrens' house had all the shades drawn, not uncommon in a mourning household, but still at once sad and forbidding. Amanda rang the bell and a maid wearing a black armband ushered her into the sitting room. Kitty jumped up and took Amanda by both hands.

"Things are bad. Come sit down." They moved over to the sofa and Kitty continued, "Remember in March when President Roosevelt declared a week-long bank holiday? Everything shut down for a week with the banks closed. That was the beginning of the trouble. My father lost a lot of money and he decided to sell the Turner painting. My uncle had been pestering him for years about it and so they set about doing that."

"They owned it jointly?" Amanda asked, although she knew it was the case from reading Gilbert's notes.

"Yes, it was the last of what was once an extensive collection. I guess they were selling things off from time to time and it was finally going to be the end of the Warren art collection. Uncle August is the younger brother and frankly has a chip on his shoulder that my father got Belvedere. He got the use of the house, of course, but it belonged to my father."

"Will he inherit the house, do you think?"

"I'm sure of it. I haven't seen the will or anything, but it's been in the family for so long and passed from father to son or brother to brother. How could it not be his?"

They sat in silence for a while before Kitty spoke again. "They're bringing Daddy home tomorrow and we'll have the funeral at the end of the week."

"Do you need any help with that?"

"I think we'll manage but I'd like you to be here. For moral support."

"Of course."

"Next week I'll have to go to Hyannis and pack up our personal things. I know you're busy at work...."

"Actually, no, I'm not. But that's another story."

"Then would you consider going down to the Cape with me and my mother next week to deal with things? Sorting and packing?"

"Of course. I'm the big organizer, remember?"

The house had been quiet except for a distant telephone ringing. A few moments later, they heard a scream. Kitty shot up and raced to a back room with Amanda at her heels.

"It's Mother. In the library," she said as they ran down a hallway.

Kitty stopped in the doorway before making her way quickly to her mother, seated at a desk, the telephone receiver still in her hand.

"What is it?" Kitty asked.

"Things have gone from terrible to horrible."

She crouched next to her mother. "What do you mean?"

Mrs. Warren gnawed on her bottom lip trying to pluck up her courage. "The police from Hyannis called. The doctor said Rupert didn't die from a heart attack. He was poisoned."

"How? I mean, with what? I'm sorry, I shouldn't be asking," Amanda said as Kitty seemed too stunned to speak.

"With arsenic," Mrs. Warren said in a whisper. "It wasn't an accident. It was intentional. Someone killed him."

Chapter 7

"But who, why? Daddy didn't have any enemies!" Kitty shouted, standing up.

Mrs. Warren stood up to embrace her daughter but quickly went limp, collapsing into her daughter's arms.

"Let's get her over to the loveseat," Amanda said, taking up the woman's feet while Kitty held her mother by the torso. It was an awkward shuffle across the room to place her on her back.

"Are we supposed to put her head up or down?" Kitty asked.

"I know what to do. Go get help. I'll see to your mother." Amanda put two cushions under Mrs. Warren's legs ensuring that her lower body was higher than her head and loosening the scarf around her neck. She felt her torso to check if she had some kind of corset on, not that many women still wore them, and began to pat the woman's hands to revive her. She was pale and breathing shallowly but steadily. Footsteps thundered in the hallway and Kitty preceded a stout maid who looked as though she could carry her employer upstairs by herself.

"Can you call your doctor? I think she's only just fainted. Smelling salts would be good."

Kitty went to the desk and dialed the telephone while the maid ran out of the room and Amanda continued to pat the hands of the woman who was still unconscious. In less than a minute the maid came back with a bottle of vinegar and, taking off the top, put it beneath Mrs. Warren's nose.

Kitty got through to the doctor who lived just a few houses down and, while she quickly told him the issue, Mrs. Warren coughed and turned her head away from the smell.

"Stop, stop!" she managed to say.

The maid gave a bit of a smile and Amanda looked at her. "Good thinking! Now, for some brandy?"

The maid handed the vinegar bottle to Amanda, then went over to a set of books that were piled on top of each other on a nearby bookshelf. She brought the adjoined volumes over to the desk and lifted the top. While they may have once been books, they had been glued together and concealed a compartment that contained a small decanter and four shot glasses. She poured the brandy into one of the glasses and gave it to Amanda to offer to Mrs. Warren.

"He has me refill the decanter as needed," the maid said referring to Mr. Warren. She nodded toward the decanter indicating that she could pour Amanda a glass, but it was refused.

"What's your name?"

"Aldona."

"Mine's Amanda. Nice to meet you. You've been a lifesaver."

The woman flushed with pleasure. "I'd better get to the sitting room and wait for the doctor."

With bag in hand, he must have run the short distance from his house and was ushered into the study where Mrs. Warren was upright, having insisted that she not be prone with her legs in the air, as she put it.

"Doctor Clifton, she just got some bad news and I think that caused a fainting spell," Kitty said.

The doctor was busy taking her pulse and checking her heart rate with his stethoscope before turning to Kitty and saying, "If it was a shock, I think she'll be fine soon. Please, no more excitement or exertion. Can you step outside for a moment and fill me in?"

Amanda stayed with Mrs. Warren while Aldona stood nearby in case she was needed.

"I'd like to get up," Mrs. Warren said although she was persuaded not to do so until the doctor returned. The look on his face showed that Kitty had told him everything and he agreed that the patient could be put to bed if she had assistance going up the stairs.

Aldona and Kitty took Mrs. Warren between them and slowly proceeded out of the room to get her to her bedroom. The doctor looked at Amanda and shook his head. "This is a bad business. What do we know of what happened to Rupert?"

"Just what Mrs. Warren said after the telephone call. How could he be poisoned?"

"If it was arsenic, I'm sorry to say it is still available and used for rat infestations although tightly controlled. The public has been made aware of the dangers for years. It can be mistaken for other substances since it is odorless and tasteless, but the modern distributors of raticide use colorant to alert the user that it is not flour or sugar. Still, older versions may be lying about in sheds or garages." He shook his head. "It's a painful way to die, and I'm saddened to hear it."

"I understand that his body is to be returned tomorrow," Amanda said.

"The sooner they get the funeral arranged and in motion, the better. And I count on your discretion not to share this information with anybody. Most especially not the newspapers."

"Of course not," Amanda said, put out that he should even think that of her.

"I'll let myself out," he said, and she stood awkwardly in the study wondering if she should follow, then reconsidered and went upstairs and sought out Mrs. Warren's room. It was easy to find because Aldona was standing guard in the hall outside the slightly open door.

"Excuse me," Amanda said. "Could you ask Kitty to step out for a moment?"

Kitty came out, her face pinched with worry. "He's given her a sedative."

Amanda took her hands. "I should probably leave. But please call me if you want to talk or need any help with the arrangements."

"Thank you, dear friend. I'll need to call my uncle. I'm sure he'll want to take charge of things and I'm more than happy to leave it to him."

Amanda drove home with her shoulders in a knot. Opening the car's window, she thought the cold air might revive her, but it seemed oppressive, and the slightest wind seemed like an assault. Walking up the back stairs in her house, her only thought was taking a bath and getting into bed. If only she had taken a shot of that brandy.

Her mother was in the sitting room when she came in and stood up at once, sensing from her daughter's posture that something was wrong.

"What is it?"

"It's awful. Mrs. Warren just learned that her husband was poisoned."

Mrs. Burnside clapped her hand over her mouth and sat abruptly. "How horrible."

"I'm not supposed to say anything to anybody, but, of course, family doesn't count," Amanda added.

"How in the world could something like that happen?" Her mother gave it more thought. "I don't like to say it, but some of those Cape residents resent the folks who only visit in the summer."

Amanda remained standing. "I'll have someone bring tea." She went to the kitchen and found Mary talking to Cook. Both noticed something was amiss although nothing was said.

"I don't know the circumstances of what happened," Amanda said on her return to the sitting room.

"Nothing like that has ever happened in our beach house community in Maine," her mother said, forgetting about events of the past year. "But then again, it seems that people with money bought up the best properties right along the water in Hyannis. Not like our place where you must hike down a path to a rocky beach."

"I haven't been able to find out what else he might have been doing down there at this time of year. It seems like a long trip when he could have given instructions to the staff by telephone."

"What's to become of poor Mrs. Warren?

The tea came in as Mr. Burnside arrived home from work. He noticed the somber atmosphere at once but waited until Mary had left the room and he had removed his hat and coat.

"What's going on?"

Amanda related what she knew, and he was as shocked as she and her mother had been.

"He was a well-liked man." After a moment's thought, he added, "There had been some financial difficulties recently, however."

"You're not suggesting he took his own life!" Mrs. Burnside said.

"No, not at all. And men don't typically take their own lives with poison."

Amanda remembered Brendan mentioning once that poison was a 'woman's weapon,' and although she recoiled at the notion that it implied cowardice in its application, she didn't have enough information to refute his statement.

"Do others know this?" Mr. Burnside asked.

"Just the family here, Doctor Clifton, and whoever discovered it when they examined the body there." She shuddered.

"Let's be careful not to say anything to anyone. And I'm sorry to suggest that we leave Louisa out of the conversation as well."

Mrs. Burnside looked up sharply.

"She is out and about with many people during the day, and I don't know how discreet she would be. After all, she only knows the Warrens through Amanda and that sort of salacious information could have some appeal to the people she associates with."

Amanda agreed entirely but was surprised at her father's bald statement about her sister and her friends.

"I think she can be trusted, but if you insist…." Mrs. Burnside said, letting her doubts hang in the air.

"I've had a bit of a rough day between the Warrens' difficulties and what's going on at the hospital. I think I'll take two aspirin and lie down for a bit," Amanda said leaving her parents in the dark about what else may have occurred.

There never came a time for them to ask since she slept through dinner and the next day was full on duty with Kitty, helping her make decisions about her father's funeral. They had sat in the dining room of the Warrens' house discussing possible hymns when they heard footsteps coming from the sitting room. Looking up, Amanda was shocked to see Mr. Warren in the doorway, only to realize a moment later that it must be his brother.

"Uncle August," Kitty wailed as she ran up to him. "Where have you been? We've been trying to call you."

The resemblance to the deceased Mr. Warren was striking, mostly in their size and coloring, but once he spoke, his mannerisms were entirely different from the man that Amanda had known.

"I was up at the cabin hunting until this morning. It wasn't until I checked in at my office that I learned what had happened. I rushed over as soon as I changed."

Kitty introduced her friend and after condolences and tears were shed, she explained what they had been doing before his entrance. While still standing, he took charge immediately, quizzing Kitty about whether the church had been reserved, the bishop invited to preside (but he would be out of town), the pallbearers selected, the seating outlined, the reception location and menu chosen, and the casket picked out. It was done so rapidly and with such precision that he overlooked her sensitive state that collapsed when he mentioned the word 'casket.'

"Yes, all that has been done," Kitty said, holding back tears.

Amanda went to her friend and put an arm around her. "Mr. Warren," she said, "this has been difficult."

"I'm sorry. Kitty, you know me—I have to handle things methodically and logically. If I let my emotions out…." He cleared his throat and sat down. "Please excuse what must seem like a lack of feeling. You know your father and I were like peas in a pod growing up."

He turned to Amanda and explained. "We're only two years apart. Birthdays in the same month even."

Kitty blew her nose in a handkerchief and took a deep breath to calm herself. "Well, then, let me tell you what I have been able to do so far."

Amanda was proud of her friend's strength in the face of a formidable relative and admired how she had organized almost all the details on her own. After she had shown him what she had done, he apologized for being abrupt and they embraced, all tension forgotten.

"Have you seen Mother yet?" Kitty asked.

"No, I wanted to get a sense from you of how she is holding up."

"It's been terrible for her. She's upstairs; go on up, she'll be happy to see you."

After he left, Amanda realized she knew nothing about Kitty's uncle. "Is he in business with your father?"

"No, not at all. He's an architect in practice by himself. The sunporch addition on the Hyannis house was his design."

"I always thought that was part of the original building," Amanda said.

"He's quite good. And as you can see, he's exacting. From what my father said, he had to select all the hardwood, insisted on specific paint colors for the room and even the furniture."

"A thorough person. Is he married?"

"Why? Are you interested?" Kitty asked with the first smile she had produced that day.

"Of course not. You know all about Brendan. I just wondered if you had any cousins."

"No, not yet. He shows up at events with a different beautiful woman on his arm each time, but I don't think he wants to get tied down. Although he may need to get a wife sometime soon, since he's going to inherit the Belvedere."

Although Amanda had already agreed to help the Warrens pack up, she thought it was going to be a melancholy task just before Christmas. What she didn't expect was that it would become treacherous as well.

Chapter 8

The next days unfolded in a blur of activity. Mr. Barlow handed in his resignation and Amanda asked Mrs. Tyrell, the Board Chair, for a week off to help Kitty and Mrs. Warren with everything. The funeral was well attended, the reception held at their house well organized and executed although Amanda was surprised that August acted as if he had arranged the entire thing. It had become common knowledge that the will stipulated that he get the Hyannis house, and if people weren't familiar with the situation, they might have thought that he had inherited the Beacon Hill house, too, by the way he seemed to take charge of everything. Mrs. Warren held up well throughout though she felt animosity towards her brother-in-law, who, in the opinion she voiced privately to her daughter, didn't seem too distressed by his older brother's death.

Once the last guest had left the reception, the caterers packed up the food and removed their serving dishes, glasses and plates. Mrs. Warren, Kitty, August and Amanda went to the sitting room, each with a glass of sherry.

"Here's to Rupert," August said, and they raised their glasses and took a drink. "I understand you're going down to Belvedere to pack up some of your personal items," he said.

"Yes, we're leaving tomorrow. I'd rather deal with it sooner than later. Amanda is coming to help."

"How nice of her. I might be going down in the next day or so myself. I'd be happy to assist."

The look on Mrs. Warren's face said more than her vague comment of, "You don't have to bother."

"No, it would be my pleasure to assist. There is so much stuff in that house!" He gave a slight chuckle. "Have you been up in the attic recently?"

"No, as a matter of fact. I understood some of the things up there belonged to your grandmother."

"And some generations before, too, I'm sure. Trunks and cupboards full of what not."

Amanda was put off by his cheerful demeanor, which came across as gloating at having inherited such a fine property even if it included 'stuff' and 'what not.'

"I meant to ask, do you know if Rupert ever upgraded the electric?" he asked.

Mrs. Warren stared at him. "I really couldn't say. That was his bailiwick. I did the furnishings and the gardens." Her defiant look suggested that he better not think about neglecting her years of effort or tearing up the rose bushes.

Kitty broke in, "It sounds like the caterers are almost finished. I'll go see," and she got up, as did Amanda, uncomfortable with the tension in the room.

"Did someone pay them yet?" August called out.

"As if he would pull out his wallet to do so," Kitty muttered to her friend as they walked to the kitchen. "Of course, we've got that all sorted."

The man who seemed to be the head of the catering team nodded in her direction. "I think we've got everything. If we've left something behind, let us know and someone can swing by in the next few days and pick it up." He shook hands with both young women and nodded solemnly to them both. The kitchen back door closed, and the house was silent.

"I wish he would leave already," Kitty said.

"Does he have a house here in town?"

"He has an apartment here and rents—or should I say, used to rent—a small house in Barnstable. He had to vacate and rents a room now. I wonder if he even has enough money to pay for the upkeep on Belvedere. Heating the place costs a fortune; it's one reason we never went down in the winter."

"Who looks after the place when you're not there?"

"Josiah is the gardener and handyman and he's on call to deal with mechanical things. Gertrude is the housekeeper during the fine weather and in the winter, she stops in daily to check on things. She heats up the stove to warm the kitchen and then makes the rounds of the rooms to make sure everything is locked up and no critters or humans are taking up residence."

"Do you mean squatters?" Amanda could not imagine such a thing.

"It's happened from time to time. Not in our house, thank goodness. Poor people and hobos looking for shelter in the cold weather." Kitty drank down the rest of her sherry and put the glass in the sink. "Staff will be in tomorrow to clean up the rest, although there isn't much to clean up. I could see Cook was put out at not having been asked to prepare the entire reception. Frankly, I thought it would be too much effort and she's not getting any younger. And I didn't want to have to deal with any tantrums on her part if things didn't go as she wanted. It was better she was a guest mourner and now everyone is gone."

"Well, I'd better be going myself," Amanda said, noting that it was almost dark.

Kitty gave her a hug. "Thank you for everything. And you'll be ready by late morning to go down to the Cape?"

"Yes. I'll bring my warmest clothes and be ready to do whatever needs doing."

"You're a pal."

EVEN THOUGH AMANDA had just seen her parents at the Warrens' house, they seemed surprised that she had returned so soon.

"Dear, you look exhausted," Mrs. Burnside said, patting the seat on the sofa next to her so her daughter could sit.

"That was draining."

"Funerals are like that," her father said. He was seated closest to the fireplace and checked to see that there was enough wood to feed it. "I understand that the brother got the house in Hyannis. He didn't get the house in town, too, did he?"

"No. Kitty told me it was her father's sole property. By the way he was surveying everything, you'd think he had his eye on it, too."

Mr. Burnside raised his eyebrows. "August always did have lofty ambitions when it came to acquisitions. Not so much toward work, however."

"Kitty told me he was an architect. They do well, don't they?"

"With the Crash, everyone has tightened their belts, but he was treading water before that. He used to work with a large firm but was a bit too imposing of his own ideas on the clients, which doesn't go well in that line of work. You're there to meet the clients' needs, not insist on your concept of what their primary residence should look like. He's not Frank Lloyd Wright, after all."

Louisa came breezing in, still in her hat and coat with the canvas portfolio case under her arm.

"Hello, all!" she said. "Sorry I couldn't attend the Warren thing, but Monsieur Josef wanted me to see the rough model of the two dresses I had designed. My, those seamstresses do wonders with their nimble fingers. They managed to get some scraps of silk and it made the design drape beautifully."

"Would it help for you to get more training? Like in New York?" her mother asked.

Amanda hid a smile, knowing that she was still thinking of a way to separate Louisa from Rob.

"What are the best places in New York for that?" Mrs. Burnside asked.

Mr. Burnside and Amanda shrugged their shoulders.

"There's the New York School of Fine and Applied Art in Manhattan. And," Louisa said with emphasis, "it has a branch in Paris."

Her father made a grumbling sound as he envisioned his younger daughter's intention of getting a European sojourn at his expense.

"If you attended in New York, you could live with your aunt and uncle in Pelham," Mrs. Burnside said with enthusiasm.

"And commute into the City?" Louisa asked as if she would have to walk all the way. "It would be so much more fun to share a place with some other girls."

Mr. Burnside turned his attention to the fireplace while his wife and daughter sketched out her exciting life away from home. Putting the tongs back in their holder he turned to say, "You are aware that this country is in a Depression, aren't you? And we are not immune to it although you wouldn't know by the way you spend money."

Louisa looked shocked. "I don't," she said. "Spend money, that is."

"Well, you don't earn any."

"Not yet. Not like my sister."

Amanda kept quiet, not having told her parents about the full extent of the Barlow debacle, as she termed it to herself.

"It's time to let you know how things stand before you have your daydreams of Paris or whatever. We own this house outright as well as the beach house. I earn a good salary as a partner of the firm and that sustains us. But what investments we once had are not in good shape. And I'm sorry to say that the trust funds that your grandparents set up for you have plummeted in value."

"What do you mean?" Louisa asked.

"I don't want to quote figures at this time but you both should know that their value has dropped precipitously."

Louisa sagged her shoulders. "Goodbye to that apartment," she said.

"What apartment?" Mrs. Burnside asked.

"Louisa had a daydream that I would rent an apartment and she would live with me."

Louisa turned her head and glared at her sister.

"Over my dead body!" Mr. Burnside said, his face like thunder.

"What's wrong with living with your parents until you get married? That's what I did," his wife added in a hurt tone.

"Times are changing. No, times *have* changed," Louisa said.

"And what's this about moving to Hartford?" Mr. Burnside said, directing an angry face at Amanda.

"I never said I was moving there. It was just that Mr. Barlow offered me a job as his assistant there and I told him no thank you."

Mr. Burnside crossed his legs and said, "I'm glad of that. I wouldn't want people to think you were chasing after him. Or he was chasing after you."

"Daddy, really. Nobody would think that." But knowing her parents' social group and human nature, Amanda thought it might be likely there would be gossip.

Mary stood in the doorway, unsure whether to break into the conversation, but catching the eye of her employer, she announced that dinner was ready.

"I should tell you that I'm taking some days off work to accompany Kitty to the house in Hyannis to help pack up some things," Amanda said as they went to the dining room.

"That's nice of you, dear," her mother said, hooking her arm in her daughter's."

"I just hope the change of scene will do her good and that visiting the house won't be a melancholy remembrance."

Chapter 9

At her father's urging, Amanda agreed to take two boxes of the errant investigator's papers with her on her trip to Hyannis. She thought she could assist Kitty and her mother during the day and might be able to work on them in the evening. Not that she could make much more sense out of it all, but it could be a distraction. As she lugged them to the front door, Kitty laughed for the first time in days.

"We're meant to move things out, not in."

"Just some homework my father has put me up to," Amanda said. "And do you have so little in the house to bring back that it will fit in the trunk of your car?"

"Don't be silly. We're just meant to sort things out into packing barrels that someone has delivered there. Movers will take them later. And we don't have to go through everything on this trip. I'll see how Mother handles things and we'll stay as long as she wants. Or doesn't want."

Mrs. Warren was in the passenger seat, bundled up in a sweater, wool pants, boots and fur coat, making Amanda wonder if the heat was working at the house on the Cape.

After all, the family never went in the winter and perhaps there wasn't central heating.

"I'll just be a few more minutes," Amanda said, returning to her room and pulling two more sweaters from her dresser, bringing them and the last carton of Gilbert papers to the car.

It was such a different-looking vista driving south through a wintery landscape. Amanda had visited the Warrens when she was young, before Kitty had gone off to school and her father had taken positions abroad. Now she wondered if she would recognize any of it—the house, the beach, the town. There was little traffic, just locals going about their usual daily business rather than the line of cars that defined summer weekends. How sad it must be for Kitty and her mother to realize the finality of this last visit. Somehow Amanda got the impression that August wasn't going to be generous with his invitations to his sister-in-law, nor would she be looking forward to seeing him take possession of what she still felt was her house.

"Right about here is when we would roll down the windows and sniff the air to tell if we could smell the ocean, remember, Mother?"

Mrs. Warren smiled. "Yes, it was like having a puppy in the car. You would always put your head out, close your eyes and let the wind blow your hair all about."

Kitty gave a laugh. "Come on, Amanda, let's give it a try. We're almost to the bridge."

"Certainly not," Amanda replied, trying to sound stuffy. "Not only will my hat go flying off my head into the marsh, but it must be subzero outside."

"Let's see," Kitty said, rolling down her window as she drove.

"Be careful," her mother said and added a moment later, "Amanda is right. It's winter and it is near freezing. I hope Gertrude or Josiah has had the sense to turn on the heat."

Kitty obeyed her mother while Amanda was relieved that there was warmth to be had at the house.

"If she's forgotten, we can always camp out in the sitting room in front of a roaring fire," Kitty said.

"That's if Josiah has enough in the woodpile."

"Let's look on the bright side, Mother. We've had wonderful years at the house and now we'll say goodbye."

Mrs. Warren didn't look as if she saw any sort of bright side to the situation and said nothing in response.

Once over the bridge, there were signs of habitation, if only a Shell station, complete with its giant frieze of a scallop shell in front of the portico.

"Does your family still have the beach house in Maine?" Mrs. Warren asked.

"Yes. It's small and quiet but a good escape from the city."

"Must be nice," she said in a small voice.

As they continued, well set back from the main road they were on, clapboard houses began to appear, their formerly green lawns littered with the remains of fallen autumn leaves and soon to be covered in snow. Amanda remembered that Bostonians referred to people on the Cape almost as if they were another breed of humanity. Tough, a bit stern and difficult to understand. Surely that was just a stereotype.

"These houses are lovely," she said, imagining herself in a warm room behind the rippled glass windows looking out at the elm trees that lined the road. Her head swiveled from side to side, taking it all in as Kitty slowed down to accommodate the older vehicles on the road and then crawled along after a tractor.

"Why do they insist on coming on to the main roads and holding everyone up?" Kitty asked.

"You're sounding just like a city person."

"Well, I am." She shook her head at Amanda's response.

"There's been some friction between the people who live here permanently and those who come only for the summer season."

"They call themselves 'year-roun-dahs,'" Kitty said with a giggle.

"Now, now," her mother chided.

"They think they are tougher because they make it through the winter, as if Boston were some tropical paradise by comparison. I should say that they think we are hopelessly feeble physically. Josiah, the gardener-handyman who is paid to chop wood, mow the lawn and fix things, has an unpleasant, superior face whenever he's asked to help. Don't you think, Mother?"

"I don't pay attention to his whims. He does what he's told, and he's been with us for years."

"Do you think Uncle August will keep him on?"

Her mother sighed and looked out the window. "I really couldn't say."

Amanda wondered how it was that Kitty complained about the man yet seemed concerned about his future job prospects.

"Is there enough for him to do in the winter?" Amanda asked.

"Rupert worked out an interesting arrangement with him. He's paid as if he works all year round although there is significantly less to do in the winter, but so much more is required of him when the family is here."

"Lots of fetching of food, fixing the car, taking care of the boat, that sort of thing," Kitty explained.

The tractor pulled off the road onto a track that led to a barn in the distance.

"Finally!" Kitty said as she accelerated.

In some places there were guest houses along the road along with shops, then open land with bare trees before residential areas came up again. Amanda looked from side to side, fascinated by the clapboard houses before seeing a small sign indicating they had entered another town although everything looked the same. There weren't many stoplights to interrupt traffic through the town centers that had a few shops, restaurants and a gas station.

"I really don't remember much of my previous trip here," Amanda said. "Maybe because I was smaller and couldn't see out the windows as well. In any case, I wouldn't have been as charmed by the houses as I am now."

"Yes, this is a pretty village. Some of our Beacon Hill neighbors have a place around here."

"Who is that?" Kitty asked.

"I can't remember just now," her mother responded and looked out the window again.

"We're coming into Hyannis now, Amanda. Big town here."

The road they had been on became the main street of the town, lined with stores, a post office, and two-story brick buildings that may have housed offices for professional people.

The locals needed dentists and doctors and lawyers just as anybody else might. They stopped at what might have been the only traffic light in town, and Kitty pointed out a clothing store that took up a good portion of the street.

"If you didn't bring enough warm clothing, that's the place to go. All extremely tasteful, of course. If you want a hat with flannel earflaps, there's always the hardware store," Kitty said.

"That sounds like a charming accessory, but I think I'll leave it to the lumberjacks to popularize it."

The light changed and they drove several more blocks before turning right and following the commercial street that soon became residential before reaching a T in the road and turning right again, then quickly left onto a gravel road marked 'Private.' Either side of the pathway was lined with white pickets for some hundred yards before opening up to what must have been in summer a vast lawn. A young man was walking away from the house as they came to the end of the driveway.

"Who's that?" Amanda asked.

"It looks like Daniel, Gertrude's son."

Kitty pulled the car up to the house rather than the nearby garage to unload their luggage and she honked the horn.

"I wish you wouldn't do that," her mother said, getting out of the passenger side.

"Josiah will never hear us otherwise. Or pretend not to know we're here until we've lugged all the bags in ourselves." Kitty got out and walked to the back door, found it unlocked and went in, leaving the door wide open.

Mrs. Warren shook her head and followed, Amanda bringing up the rear.

Passing through the mud room, once they got into the kitchen of the house, they were overcome with the sad silence of the place broken only by the noise of a kettle coming to a boil on the stove top. It shrieked as the steam came out of the nozzle and Kitty lunged over to turn off the gas. Just then, the swinging door at the other end of the room burst open and a middle-aged woman appeared with a shocked look on her face.

"Lordy, you startled me, Mrs. Warren," she said, her hand to her chest.

"Gertrude, you knew we were coming," Mrs. Warren replied.

"Yes, but...I don't know why I was startled. I'm sorry. I've been jumpy lately. Here, I was just about to make some tea. You must be tired and cold from your trip."

"The car has a heater, you know, and it wasn't that long a journey," Mrs. Warren said, not looking at the other woman but taking her gloves off, finger by finger, while looking around the kitchen. "This room could use a lick of paint, but, oh, well...." She drifted off, remembering that it wouldn't be her problem anymore.

"Where's Josiah?" Kitty asked. "We need him to bring in the bags. You remember Amanda, don't you?"

The older woman tilted her head to one side and thought. "It must have been a long time ago."

"Yes, I was probably about ten years old. So, I'm glad you don't recognize me. I'd be crushed if you had said I hadn't changed a bit."

That brought what passed for a smile to the woman's face as she sidled past Kitty and went to the cupboards to get out the tea things. While she rattled around, Mrs. Warren pushed through the door into the hallway and slowly walked through the quiet rooms. Kitty stayed in the warm kitchen, not wanting to intrude on her mother's feelings, and Amanda had that awkwardness of the new guest not knowing what to do just then.

Instead, she walked out toward the car and then changed direction and went around the back of the house to the broad lawn where they had played croquet as children, now covered in a light dusting of snow. Unlike other memories, the expanse of the property seemed larger than she remembered, with the neighboring homes on either side separated by a line of evergreen trees. She only had ankle-high boots on so didn't take the long walk down the sloping turf to the beach.

Amanda brought the first two suitcases into the kitchen, wondering why Kitty and her mother had packed so much for a short stay. She repeated the process bringing in her own suitcase and train case just in time to see Josiah appear from somewhere inside the house.

"I could have done that," he said.

"Yes, but you didn't," Gertrude replied.

She had a full tray of the tea things along with slices of poppy seed cake and a smug look on her face that indicated it must have been a family favorite. Amanda preceded her through the swinging door, holding it open for her, then following the woman down the hall and into the dining room. It had been so long since she had been there that she hadn't quite remembered where everything was. But the first glimpse of the toile wallpaper gave her a smile as if she were still that young girl enamored of seeing how other people decorated their houses.

"Thank you, Gertrude, my favorite," Kitty said. Her mother was still, taking in the surroundings, perhaps thinking these might be the last few days that she would be able to enjoy them. The likelihood that August would invite them in the future was slim, and the notion that they would accept was out of the question.

"Not much has changed," Amanda said, sitting down and then immediately regretted her comment because, of course, for the Warrens everything had changed. But, to her relief, neither woman reacted negatively to her remark.

"Gertrude does make the best poppy seed cake," Kitty said, attempting to get her mother to say something, to no avail.

"There doesn't seem to have been much snow yet," Amanda said, knowing that to talk about the weather was safe ground.

"That's all that's left," Gertrude said, still standing beside the table. "It was quite a storm. You know what the Farmer's Almanac says about such things." She didn't elaborate and left with Kitty and Amanda looking at each other silently, wondering what that premonition meant.

They had their tea in silence until Mrs. Warren sighed and said she was tired and was going to lie down for a bit.

"Are the rooms ready?" Kitty asked.

"That is my expectation after having called to let Gertrude know we were coming down." She pushed herself away from the table and, still in her outerwear and hat, left the room. The young women looked at one another as if to ask if they should look in on her but neither one said a word. Amanda was beginning to regret taking on this task for her friend.

Once they finished their tea, Amanda took the luggage upstairs as Josiah was nowhere to be seen. She tapped on what she thought must be Mrs. Warren's door since it was the only room with the door closed, and hearing a response, put the cases just inside the door. Returning downstairs, she took own baggage while Kitty took hers and they lugged them up the staircase.

"Here's your room," Kitty said, pointing to the one nearest the stairs. The bathroom is between yours and mine."

Amanda remembered the last time she had been there they had shared a room. Well, that was when they were young and giggly and these days there was not much to laugh about. Amanda unpacked and sat on the bed before deciding to get a pair of high boots from the mud room and explore outside before it became dark. Luckily, there were many pairs of rubber boots and once pulled on, she became excited to see what the yard, the dock and the beach looked like compared to her memory of them.

The wind had picked up, but she bundled her scarf more tightly around her neck and walked in a straight line from the back porch toward the beach. The trees that were meant to delineate the properties did not extend as far down to the water, of course, which allowed her to see not only the houses on either side, but the entire string of summer homes from one end of the curved bay to the other. Her memory might have been faulty or perhaps she hadn't paid much attention as a young child, but it seemed there were no longer empty stretches of beachfront. The houses had a similarity in structure and design expected in this location, although some seemed to have taken up more than just one lot. She wondered when all this development had taken place —surely not in the years since the Crash—and who or what money had been able to create it.

Amanda walked down to the beach and looked at the white-caps rolling in, remembering splashing in the water and squealing every time a wave hit. They had been little waves but seemed huge back then. Down to her left was the small dock from which they had jumped into the water and where a sailboat was tied up in the summer. The boat was gone, likely stowed away in the barn for the season and she wondered who had been making use of it all these years. Certainly not Mr. Warren, who was often abroad, and not Kitty, who liked being a passenger but was too timid to command the vessel herself.

A gull squawked overhead and disappeared into the distance. She walked farther down the beach and saw the grand empty houses, awaiting the change of seasons for their owners to come back. As a game, Amanda decided to see how far she could walk along the sand before seeing another human being. It was almost a half mile before she came across an older man walking his white muzzled Labrador.

"All locked up here," he said in the unmistakable Cape accent before continuing on his way.

She turned to watch him in his steady stride before realizing that her feet were cold and deciding to go back. As she came in sight of the house, she saw Josiah was hauling a moving barrel in through the back door. Having lived in the same house all her life, Amanda had no idea that this was how things were packed and transported. Catching up to him, she held the door open, for which he thanked her as he rolled the heavy cardboard barrel through the kitchen and hallway into the dining room and stood it next to half a dozen others.

Kitty was already in the room with the china cabinet doors open, taking down the dinner service piece by piece, while Gertrude wrapped each one in newspaper and carefully laid it into the nearest barrel, well cushioned with towels.

"I thought I'd get a good head start before Mother got up from her nap. Packing up a lifetime, really."

"I'd be happy to help, but just let me get out of my outer clothes," Amanda said, returning to the mud room to hang up coat, scarf and knitted hat. When she got back and saw the daunting task ahead of them, she said, "Kitty, do you mind me looking around the house? I haven't been here in so long I wonder if I'll remember anything."

"You've convinced me," Kitty said. "Let's explore."

Gertrude put down the dish she had picked up. "I'm not going to do this all by myself. I've got chores in the kitchen," and she wiped her hands on her apron, scowled and left the room.

"Oops," Amanda said.

"Don't pay any attention to her. Just an old grump. Let's start in the sitting room," she suggested. "I don't think it has changed much in the past century." They went through the doorway into the large room that faced the front garden edged with evergreen shrubs, the dormant grass partly covered with leaves and a distant brick wall that shielded the house from the street view.

"I don't remember this at all. It's a lovely room," Amanda said.

"You wouldn't. Children weren't generally allowed in it. Adults only unless they wanted me to come in and say hello to somebody or other and be gone. I've always loved the light blue upholstery—such a soothing room. But everything in here is silk, another reason I was seldom allowed in."

"It's very formal." Amanda walked to the windows and, orienting herself, realized that the part of the house she had been most familiar with was the back inside porch that led out to the expansive grass lawn that finally gave way to the beach.

"There's the dreaded music room," Kitty said. "They even had me take piano lessons in the summer, of all things."

Amanda remembered there were many people in the house when she had stayed and at one point in their playtime, Kitty was called away for her lessons.

"Do you still play?" Amanda asked, walking into that room that contained a grand piano and easy chairs in conversational groupings.

"No. I was always more interested in looking out the windows. You can see whoever is coming up to the front door from here. It used to drive my piano teacher crazy." She giggled and opened the keyboard and played a few chords. "Ugh. Terribly out of tune." She closed it again.

"I'll bet you never saw my father's study, either," Kitty said.

"I wouldn't know. I doubt it."

"I bet your father has one, too. All pipe smoke and leather chairs. He might as well have had a sign on the door, 'No girls allowed.'"

They peeked in the room, and it was just as Kitty had described it down to the faint odor of tobacco. Dark wood furniture, a leather couch, books lining the walls and some letters on the desk. Kitty took one, looked at the return address, then another and put them down.

"I guess we'll have to deal with all that sometime soon," she said, leaving the room quickly.

The one wall without bookcases had a low table and above it was a blank space with a slightly smaller, lighter space within it as if something had once hung there.

"The painting that you're selling?" Amanda asked.

"Yes. I don't know if you ever saw it. All hazy and fuzzy looking with ships. It was always referred to as The Painting. Off in a gallery. I suppose we should, I mean August should put something in its place. It looks so naked. Dreadful to imagine that he gets to sit in Daddy's chair." She paused only a moment before going out the door.

Down a long hall was a closed door and Amanda was sure she had never been back there, either. Kitty opened it and they were hit with a wall of windows facing north.

"My mother's studio," she said.

There was a long table with a huge piece of wood alongside sculpting tools.

"Did you mother carve that?" Amanda inquired.

"No," Kitty laughed. "It's a piece of driftwood. She retrieves them then carves and sands them into slightly different shapes. My father always referred to my mother's sculpture as her creatures. She thought it was funny. This one she called 'The Sea,' although how it depicts the ocean, I can't imagine."

Amanda walked up to the object and accepted that driftwood suggested the name the piece had been given, but what did she know of modern art? Shelving along the wall contained dozens of other pieces of worked wood of different sizes along with chisels, hammers, and instruments. What an interesting hobby, she thought. Her mother was devoted to the more usual feminine pursuits like needlepoint and pressing flowers, so this was totally unexpected.

"While we were out sailing or swimming or creating a ruckus, she would escape to her studio and hack at a piece of wood. I sometimes wonder if she wasn't getting out her anger with it."

"About what?"

"Whatever women are angry about, I guess. Being tied to home and family. I don't know if she wanted to be a sculptor—"

"But she is," Amanda corrected. "In her own way."

"I meant a successful artist. Whatever that means. So that's the tour of the inner sanctum that you never saw as a child. It was as if they thought we had chocolate on our fingers and would mar the furniture." With a laugh, she added, "They were probably right. Anyway, we had more fun romping around outside, didn't we?"

They walked back toward the dining room and saw that Gertrude had been true to her word and was crashing around in the kitchen.

"Let's get to work upstairs," Kitty suggested and, with a sigh, they went to the second floor.

Chapter 10

While Kitty and Amanda were unloading the linen cupboard, Mrs. Warren got a phone call that the sheriff and the doctor were on their way to give her more details about her husband's death. Having recently taken up smoking again, she waited in the sitting room and paced up and down waiting for the doorbell to ring. She was dreading the meeting but at least they had granted her the courtesy of coming to the house rather than having her go to the sheriff's office in town where everyone would see her and start tongues wagging.

"Do you know which are yours and which stay with the house?" Amanda asked, picking through the linen napkins upstairs.

"Of course not. To my way of thinking, everything that is here has always been here. But if we sort them into sets—which it seems Gertrude or someone has already done—my mother can determine which are ours. The monograms should be a clue since my grandfather's initials were different from my father's.

The doorbell rang and Kitty froze. She left what she was doing and went down to the sitting room to see her mother inviting two men in. They were dressed for the cold weather with thick hats with ear flaps and heavy boots, looking sheepish about the snow they had tracked in. Ever the gracious hostess, Mrs. Warren paid no attention to the puddles on the carpet, although Gertrude would have said something, and suggested they meet in the study.

"Mother, shall I go with you?" Kitty asked, being of two minds—wanting to know more but wary of learning something that she would not be able to get out of her mind later.

"No, dear," Mrs. Warren said, stubbing out the cigarette in a glass ashtray before leading the men down the hall. The study was chilly, and she regretted having chosen the location, but it afforded her the protection of sitting behind the desk and the ability to end the meeting if she so chose.

"Sheriff, I understand you have some details for me."

"Mrs. Warren, actually it is Doctor Hauck who can tell you more." He cleared his throat and looked at the other man, who clutched his hat in his hands.

"Let me express my condolences, Mrs. Warren. We've known your family and your husband's family for a long time. It was a shock and a loss to the entire community." He stopped suddenly.

"Can you provide me with more information about what happened?"

The sheriff jumped in. "At first we thought that walking through the snow drifts might have been too much of an exertion."

"Walking? He had driven down here."

"Yes, obviously. We don't know why he didn't drive into town but walked instead."

"That's rather unlike him," she said.

"He told Gertrude he had an appointment to meet someone. Knowing that he walked into town and back, however, my assumption was that he may have experienced a heart attack. That's what Gertrude said when she found him the next day and called," the doctor said.

"Not that she has any medical expertise," the sheriff added.

"And that's how it appeared to me, as well. But upon further examination when I was called in the next day to the funeral home, I saw the telltale signs of arsenic poisoning." The doctor was being purposefully vague about how he had come to that conclusion so as not to further upset the widow.

"Where had he gone into town? Did he meet someone?"

"We have scant information about that. It was early evening and already dark."

"How could someone poison him? I mean, where do you get something like that?" Mrs. Warren asked.

"You'd be surprised at what is readily available or sitting in someone's garden shed."

Mrs. Warren had so many questions she couldn't begin to articulate them.

"We know he was seen walking past the Harbisons' house, but where he was before that, we don't know."

"They live on the way into downtown, don't they?"

"Yes," the sheriff said.

"Did they mention anything odd? I still find it strange that he should walk there, especially in bad weather. Unless he couldn't drive the car for some reason."

"They didn't mention anything unusual. They said they only had a glimpse of him, recognizing his coat and hat."

She shook her head confused by the information. "And no one else saw him?"

"Not that we're aware. Your housekeeper said that she and Josiah look in daily to make sure that nothing is amiss, and although they knew your husband was here, they were shocked when they discovered him the next day."

"Of course. Mrs. Warren paused and then said, "My mind is whirling with questions but at this moment I can't articulate them." She paused. "What was he doing down here and who killed him?"

The two men looked uncomfortable and with good reason. They, too, had no idea.

Chapter 11

The young women heard talking and footsteps downstairs that they took to mean the two men were leaving. Kitty and Amanda looked at each other, but neither wanted to comment on what had happened in the study.

In a falsely bright tone, Kitty said, "Let's leave this for later. We should tackle the china cabinet." It was her way of checking on her mother without being too obvious about it. Facing the huge piece of furniture in the dining room, she said, "Ugh, I didn't realize we had so much here. Service for sixteen it looks like although I don't recall that many for a seated dinner party."

"I remember having picnics out on the terrace and the lawn," Amanda said. "Hot dogs and hamburgers."

"That was just for the children, of course. I don't remember being was invited to the adults' parties until years later."

Gertrude came in from the kitchen, wiping her hands on a dishcloth.

"They were something, Miss. Days to prepare with some girls from town helping out. People came down from Boston and spent weekends. We were busy then. But of course, I used to have more energy, too."

"You don't seem to have slowed down at all," Kitty said.

"May not look like it, but it certainly feels different. Achy in the joints, you know."

They continued taking the dishes out in silence until Gertrude held up a garish platter trimmed with painted holly around the perimeter.

"Some old friend of your father's in Boston gave this to him as a Christmas gift—big enough for a ham or turkey. Your mother disliked it so much that she brought it down here where we never used it."

"We still have that hideous thing?" Mrs. Warren said coming into the room. "Can't somebody please manage to drop it?"

"Who gave it to us anyway?" Kitty asked.

"That dreadful man—I can't remember his name—who was trying to insinuate himself into our circle just because your father had done some business with him."

"If you don't want it, Mrs. Warren, I'll be happy to take it. I think it's quite jolly," Gertrude said.

"Very well. With my good wishes to enjoy for Christmases to come."

Gertrude smiled broadly at her new acquisition.

The back door slammed, and Gertrude shook her head. "I wish Josiah wasn't so loud with his comings and goings. At least he can't sneak up on me."

But it wasn't Josiah who entered the dining room. It was August Warren, his bulk taking up most of the doorway, standing legs apart and staring at the scene in front of him.

"What in God's name do you think you're doing?" he shouted.

Mrs. Warren turned her head calmly and said, "Packing up our things."

"You mean *my* things," he said.

"No, these are ours. Rupert and I bought these for the house."

"No. They belonged to my parents."

While August's face grew redder, Mrs. Warren maintained her poise.

"Perhaps you didn't notice that the monogram is RW entwined with SW. Those were not your parents' initials." She took another plate out of the cabinet and placed it on the table.

"What happened to my parents' china?"

"It was bequeathed to your sister Dolores. Remember? When she passed away, I'm sure she left it to her daughter."

August was still puffed up with nowhere to vent his indignation. "Are you intending to empty the entire house of its belongings?"

"We'll only take what we bought and brought here."

"Are you sure you don't want to strip off the wallpaper, too?"

Mrs. Warren gave him an icy stare. "That was your mother's taste, and I wouldn't dare besmirch her memory. You're welcome to come back tomorrow to supervise the process but only on the condition that you assist."

Without another word, August turned on his heel and left, slamming the back door as he went.

"And he's not getting my plate," Gertrude said, clutching it to her chest.

～

DINNER WAS a morose affair with the specter of August's bad-tempered outburst, but after a glass of wine, Mrs. Warren seemed to relax.

"Now that your father is no longer with us, I have no compunction in telling you that I have always considered his brother a nasty man," she said.

Kitty's eyes grew wide before she let out a yelp of laughter. "Mother, I'm so glad you said that. Doesn't it feel good to finally say what everyone else has been thinking?"

Amanda kept her eyes on her plate.

"Oh, come on, Amanda. Surely there is someone in your extended family who fits the bill, too?"

She was at a loss as to how to respond and frantically searched her brain to find a likely candidate.

"You know, even one of my favorite authors, Jane Austen, always included someone either laughable or dislikeable in the immediate family. Anne's father and sister in ***Persuasion*** were hardly sympathetic characters," Kitty said.

Amanda felt more comfortable having left the personal realm and now talking of the literary. "Yes, those were the most awful folks. But she normally has silly or frivolous people in her books, a little gentler poking of fun."

"Good marks for remembering your Regency literature, but don't evade the question. Aren't there any family members you can't abide?"

"I'm sorry, I can't think of any, I did have an old-fashioned great-aunt who dressed as if she lived a hundred years ago, was hard of hearing and smelled of mothballs, but I hardly think that qualifies."

That got a small smile from Mrs. Warren and a giggle from Kitty.

"No, it doesn't, but lucky you."

It was completely dark outside as they finished their meal, Gertrude taking the plates away before returning with apple pie. The doorbell rang and she grimaced before going to answer it. The dining room's doors faced the sitting room, but from where they sat, they could not see who had come to the door. Gertrude returned and said it was Mr. Baldwin.

Mrs. Warren got up and left the room quickly.

"What brings you here?" they heard her ask him.

He took a handkerchief out of his pocket and coughed into it. "I would have come to the funeral in Boston, but I got the flu. Don't worry, I'm over it except for this blasted cough." He had removed his hat and held a briefcase in his other hand.

Kitty and Amanda followed her into the sitting room and stood beside her.

"Let me express my sincere condolences, those of my wife and family for the loss of your husband."

Mrs. Warren thought about escorting him into the study as she had the previous visitors, but there were too many of them present. "Thank you, please sit down," she said motioning to a chair. All four of them sat although Mrs. Warren wasn't sure she wanted the two young women present. She looked over at Kitty, who stood to take Mr. Baldwin's coat and hat, then put them over an ottoman rather than taking them out of the room.

"May we offer you a glass of sherry?" Kitty asked.

"No, thank you, I took the pledge long ago."

Kitty raised an eyebrow in Amanda's direction. There was an awkward silence before he began to speak again.

"I've come on family business, actually," he said, looking pointedly at Kitty and Amanda.

"They can stay," Mrs. Warren said, fearing that her husband may have had some unpaid bill with the man. Her mouth was in a tight line as if anticipating another blow.

"Your husband had consulted me about a land matter. He felt the new owners of the place next door may have encroached on your property by planting that line of trees."

Mrs. Warren sighed in relief that it was not a greater matter. "Rupert mentioned something about it. It seemed to have happened after we left in the fall."

"He authorized me to have a surveyor come out and check."

"While I could appreciate the sense of separation and privacy those trees afforded, Rupert was furious about it."

"He was correct about the encroachment. Mr. Barber was informed that the survey was to take place and he tried to prevent it. Tried running them off the property and got into a loud argument with the man as well as your husband."

"When was that?"

"About a month ago. He said it was a day trip down from the city."

Kitty and her mother exchanged glances.

"He didn't mention it."

"Perhaps he didn't want to tell you in case there was an unfortunate outcome. And for Mr. Barber there was. He was clearly in the wrong in this matter although he tried to claim adverse possession."

"What's that?" Kitty asked.

"Without going into too much detail, it means if you take and use land despite the protests of the owner over a period of time, it's yours."

"That doesn't seem fair."

"In this case, he had only planted those trees in September, so it doesn't meet the definition of duration. The whole notion is a common law practice."

"I thought common law was when two people never got married but pretended they did," Kitty said as her mother gave her a sharp look.

"Go on, Mr. Baldwin. What now?"

"Since they are on your property, you can do with them what you wish. Leave them there or cut them down."

"Cut them down? That would be a shame."

"Just to let you know, Mr. Barber thinks that for everything to be fair you should reimburse him for the cost of the trees, the labor in planting and maintaining them including the water to sustain them."

Mrs. Warren stared at Mr. Baldwin for a moment and let out a short laugh. "Of all the nerve! He can't be serious!"

"That was your husband's reaction, too, and the men had heated words about the matter."

Mr. Baldwin opened his briefcase and took out a folder. "This is the determination of the surveyor. It's important to keep hold of this. If Mr. Barber is true to form, he will try to somehow overthrow the findings."

"How can he?" Kitty asked.

"He can cause trouble in any number of ways—suggesting that the surveyor was prejudiced in your father's favor, or that as a family of some standing in Hyannis there was some sway against a newcomer. Or he could challenge the surveyor's credentials, instruments, I could go on and on."

Amanda felt that he had gone on long enough and wondered what the point was in disturbing Mrs. Warren about it.

Mrs. Warren took the folder and put it on the table beside her. "As a matter of fact, the house and property are no longer any concern of mine. I'm here to pack up some things that belong to me and I doubt Rupert's brother will be inviting me back anytime soon."

"That brings me to another matter I must discuss with you. Excuse me." He took out his handkerchief again and coughed into it. When he had finished, he looked at Kitty and Amanda in such a way that they began to sense something private or personal was about to be said.

"You girls may stay," Mrs. Warren said.

He reached into the briefcase again and withdrew another folder. "When your husband was last here, he came in and had me draw up a will."

"He already had a will," Mrs. Warren said. "Our Boston attorney read it out to us. I retain the house in Beacon Hill, its contents and our investments and August is to get this house. It's something they agreed on long ago."

Mr. Baldwin was biting his lip in discomfort. "This will supersedes the one the Boston firm prepared several years ago." He stood to hand her the folder. "This new will leaves everything, including this house, to you."

Mrs. Warren didn't move. "There must be some mistake."

"No, this is all quite legal—witnessed and signed the day he passed away as it turns out."

"But I was under the impression it was to stay in the male line."

"It may have appeared to be that way as Rupert's father inherited it from his older brother and there seemed to have been some expectation that August would next come into the property. But there was no such entailment or codicil requiring it. And your husband chose to leave his entire estate to you."

Mrs. Warren blinked but seemed unable to speak.

"That's wonderful, Mother," Kitty said.

"Yes, I suppose it is. It's such a shock. Are you sure this will is the most recent?" she asked.

"Your husband had a copy of the previous will dated some five years ago. He was adamant that he wanted to change it and that I was aware of the previous one. If I hadn't come down with the flu afterward, I would have contacted you sooner."

They looked at one another and Mrs. Warren began to cry. Kitty rushed over to her.

"See, Daddy wanted to make sure you were taken care of. That's what he was doing down here."

"I'd better be on my way," Mr. Baldwin said. Again, my condolences. Please call on me if you need any clarification or assistance." He got up and Kitty handed him his hat and overcoat while Gertrude stood at the door to the dining room trying to puzzle out what was going on.

Mr. Baldwin tipped his hat and left.

"What is August going to say?" Mrs. Warren asked.

Chapter 12

August had plenty to say the next day although how he found out so quickly no one knew. Once again, he burst in through the kitchen door and stomped his way into the dining room where Mrs. Warren and Kitty were now unpacking the barrel of china that they had filled the day before.

"What's the meaning of all this? A bogus will that yokel lawyer pulled out of his hat?"

"Won't you sit down?" Mrs. Warren asked as she carefully took the paper wrapping from a gravy boat.

"No, I won't." He stood next to the table and pounded on it. "This house was meant to be mine. Brother to brother, father to son, brother to brother."

Mrs. Warren let a few moments go by in silence to defuse the situation.

"Mr. Baldwin explained that it may have been that way over the years, but it was not legally codified," Kitty said.

Amanda was listening and observing but kept her hands busy taking wrapped pieces from the barrel.

"What do you know about the law?" August sneered at Kitty. "I'll take you to court over this." He stood fuming for a few moments but as Mrs. Warren decided not to respond, he stormed out again into the kitchen.

Mrs. Warren put her hands on the dining room table to brace herself from the recent onslaught.

"And I've always hated that hideous platter," August shouted from the kitchen. What followed was a crash and a howl from Gertrude.

"That was mine!" she cried as the back door slammed.

Kitty and Amanda ran to the kitchen to see the shattered remains of holly leaves and red berries on the floor with Gertrude hiding her face behind her hands.

"Don't worry, we'll get you another," Kitty said.

"What do you all care about me? I made countless meals and served I don't know how many banquets but all you did was make fun of me. I took pride in this house and kept it running all year round, even coming in during the winter to make sure everything is all right."

"I'm sorry, Gertrude," Kitty said, attempting to put an arm around her.

"None of you are sorry. Your family got my son put in jail for stealing and it wasn't him who pilfered the money. It was August all along. Why do you think he's been trying to make it up to me all this time with his little presents, his visits, his jokes? A phony, just like the rest of you." She slumped into a chair and wept.

Mrs. Warren had come into the room. She spoke softly. "The sheriff overreacted. Rupert never intended that he should go to jail."

ANDREA KRESS

"Well, he did, didn't he?" Gertrude said bitterly. "Ruined his life."

The women looked at each other before Gertrude left the room.

"I think we'll go home in the morning. We'll leave whatever unpacking or packing to next weekend. I want to talk to our Boston lawyer and get things straightened out," Mrs. Warren said.

"Mother, I don't like it that Uncle August just comes barging in here."

"As if he owns the place?" Mrs. Warren said wryly. "I'll have Josiah get a locksmith in to change the locks. There won't be any chance Gertrude will let him in again I don't think."

The drive back to Boston was solemn, with each woman lost in her own thoughts. Mrs. Warren's life had just been turned upside down once again and she had to come to grips with the fact that she now owned two large homes and became consumed with how she would manage to maintain them both. Is that what the sale of the painting had been all about? To raise money to keep both places up and running? Keeping Gertrude and Josiah on was the least of her worries. Who knew when the roof might need replacing or the furnace? The electrical and plumbing were as old as the house itself. Wouldn't it make more sense to put the Belvedere on the market? Then she would have enough capital to maintain her standard of living in Boston and give Kitty financial security until she married. But would Kitty be heartbroken over such a sale? Perhaps she could offer it first to August since his heart seemed set on it; that is, if he could even scrape together the money to buy it. And she had no intention of letting it go at a bargain rate.

98

Kitty's thoughts and emotions were still raw from her father's death although she had pretended to be upbeat for her mother's sake. She felt jarred by the loss of the beloved Hyannis house and then its sudden reclamation. More upsetting was her uncle's seemingly sudden and vicious reaction to events that made her feel more protective of her mother. What about her own plans to travel or move back out West where she had gone to school? Did the return of the Belvedere allow for that, or was this now one more burden for her mother to bear by herself?

Amanda's mind was on what she would return to in Boston. Was her job at the hospital still viable now that Mr. Barlow was leaving? Could she carve out some other position there, or had that phase of her life come to an end? She still had to finish the task of sorting out Mr. Gilbert's paperwork that she hadn't touched since coming to the Cape. And they were now well into December—no use looking for a job at this time of year. She'd ride things out until the New Year and make some kind of decisions then.

"We need to stop and get gas," Kitty said. "There's a place in a few miles." She pulled the car up to the pumps and an attendant came out to fill it up and check under the hood. Amanda went inside to buy a newspaper and her eyes widened as she put her money on the counter.

"Well, I never!" she said.

The owner nodded his head and smiled. "Yep. It's over."

Amanda went back to the car and held the paper up for the Warrens to see the huge headline, 'PROHIBITION OVER.'

Kitty whooped in excitement before clapping her hand over her mouth and giggling.

"You know my parents' Christmas party is this weekend. Do you think it will be a rowdy affair?" Amanda joked. The young women laughed to think of the older generation celebrating the end of an era.

"Don't think wine is going to be flowing from the Brewer Fountain downtown anytime soon," Mrs. Warren said.

ROB WORLEY, proprietor of the Oasis nightclub, had just that sort of idea. The week before, when the final state legislatures were approving the Twenty-first Amendment—the repeal of the Eighteenth, the Volstead Act—he had managed to secure a three-foot-high fountain from a shuttered restaurant. Polished and sanitized, it was ready for the red wine that would flow from the top tier down through the ornamented fish that disguised the tubes into a basin. The only drawback in the plan was its recirculating pump, which meant someone had to keep refilling the reservoir in the back while another staff person ladled the wine into glasses at the basin in the front. Rob certainly didn't want people dipping their glasses in themselves.

Louisa had stopped by to check on the preparations for the next evening and had the unusual sight of Rob without a jacket, sleeves rolled up, moving tables around with Maurice, the maître d', to allow for better flow of patrons in what was anticipated to be a busy night. Catching his eye, she moved closer for a peck on the cheek.

"Back in business, I guess," she said.

"With a bang. Good thing I stocked up weeks ago when I saw which way the wind was blowing on the vote. Can you believe that Utah was the deciding vote?"

Louisa smiled at his comment, but not being a close observer of the political scene, did not know why it was so surprising.

"Where is everybody?" she asked at the lack of staff.

"They're down at the warehouse, loading up the trucks. We hardly have room in the basement—we'll have to stash some of it in my office upstairs." He brushed his hair back with one hand. "And what have you been up to today? Have you chosen your frock yet?"

"So many decisions but I've narrowed it down to three," she laughed.

"Will Amanda and Brendan be coming?"

"I'm sure. She's on her way back from the Cape today."

"Strange time of year for a seaside vacation."

"Nothing like that. She's helping her friend sort through family items. Sad business. I'm just off to work. Gosh, it feels so important to be saying that. It's for Caroline's last fittings of her gallery outfits. They're so chic and artsy looking."

Rob tried to imagine what that meant. "Monsieur Josef will be in a good mood, I'm betting, with all the clubs moving into high gear and everyone needing to freshen up their wardrobes."

"Of course! I'd better get busy myself. I saw a new movie yesterday with my friend Cora. The clothing on the lead actress was divine. I might go back to the theater to see it with my sketchpad although I can remember most of the outfits."

"It would be money well spent. I can just see you in the dark with a flashlight taking notes."

"I don't think I would make a good spy, however. You know how I can't seem to keep secrets."

"Don't worry, your secrets are safe with me."

Chapter 13

Rob wasn't the only one who had kept secrets. Caroline Guzmán, the wife of the major investor in the Oasis who styled himself a silent partner, came from a family of wildly varying characters. Her mother, Hextilda Browne, was a known eccentric and prolific author of steamy romance novels while her brother, Fred Browne, Amanda's one-time boyfriend, was a staid and serious physician. There had been another brother, but no one spoke about that. There may also have been an illegitimate half-brother, but being a snob, Caroline would never have admitted to that, either.

When Louisa had first met Caroline, she was put off by how aloof the young woman was although she found her catty observations amusing. As she got to know her better, it seems her attitude may have been due to caution toward new acquaintances or perhaps shyness. Now that they had interacted more closely, Caroline was always bursting with gossip and tidbits about people with whom she came in contact. And Louisa, who loved to hear gossip, egged her on.

That day, the two women were having a final fitting of the somewhat outré designs that Louisa had created for someone working in an upscale art gallery. Unlike other professions, artists and people who represented them were expected to be unconventional and, while those who worked in retail were expected to appear each day in a different outfit, gallerists could wear strange and unexpected clothing and be seen in that same getup repeatedly.

Caroline had taken to the idea immediately and required three ensembles rather than the initial two: two black—of course—and one a vivid red. She felt it spoke to her inner bold creativity and would make her stand out when there was a crowd at an opening. Society matrons might attend in a smart dress or suit with fur but would never consider a dress inspired by the Cubist movement, but Louisa had a hard time convincing Caroline that some of the ideas of modern art should stay on the canvas and not in the fabric on one's back. The compromise was daring, but not strange, designs that Caroline could offset with a dramatically severe hairstyle and now an ever-present ivory cigarette holder.

As Caroline was being helped into the first dress by Louisa and a seamstress, at the ready with pins, she chatted on about the various new artists that Scofield was representing. She was adept at throwing around terms like Surrealism and rattled off names of internationally known artists—none of whom Louisa had heard of—who were at the forefront of the latest movement.

"Do stuffy Bostonians have any interest in modern art?" Louisa asked, knowing that Caroline would approve of her description of the moneyed class in their city.

"It's funny. I can tell by their expressions that they have no idea what they're looking at, but there is this sensation that if they don't jump on board the newest artistic trend, they will be seen as old school, not to mention losing out on a great profit since everyone else will be following them."

Caroline raised her arms so they could slip the dress on her. The garment was flowing without zipper or buttons in sight. The current trend in women's clothing was a defined waist, bows at the neck, busy designs and color. This dress was stark, draped in such a way as to defy expected outlines. It was a work of art.

"How do people in Boston know what might be art that is worth collecting?" Louisa asked, looking from side to side as she focused on whether the side seams should be pulled in more.

"They follow the New York market, of course. Scofield has a gallery in Manhattan, and when patrons come in to this one, he always references what is going on there."

"I'm surprised with the current financial situation that anyone is thinking about buying art."

"Louisa, there are some people whose wealth is above and beyond the recent crisis caused by the stock market crash."

Louisa had Caroline turn to the three-sided mirror to observe her creation while wondering if the woman's family or the Guzmáns were from that sort of wealth. Maybe not, or she would not be working in a gallery, but it suited her to position herself above the masses.

"This is divine! I love the way you have tapered the sleeves down to my wrists—very Renaissance." She turned to admire the side view and then the back. "Genius!"

"I would recommend being sparing in the way of accessories. Large, statement earrings, for example. We wouldn't want to detract from the flow of the dress. Dark stockings and shoes to complete the look. And perhaps your hair in a chignon as you had suggested."

"I had said that as a joke, but now I think it is necessary."

"Red lipstick, of course."

"Of course."

Louisa and the seamstress helped Caroline wiggle out of the dress and into a robe while they waited for the arrival of the next creation.

"I would think that people with money in Boston might stick to the traditional paintings. You know, ships at sea, landscapes, that sort of thing."

"That's what their parents hung on the walls. That and portraits of their forebears. It has been a task to convince them that art should not be seen as a complement to the furnishings, but something to be admired for itself. The Baileys—do you know them? New money, but they have this modern home with sleek white furniture and white walls. Perfect for modern art. You can't help but notice it on the wall and it is the centerpiece of their sitting room. Or living room, as they call it. Scofield—and he insists we call him that—no Mister or first name, you know—is trying to spearhead a trend locally and he might just succeed."

"What about all those ships and landscapes. You may want to call me old-fashioned, but it's rather soothing to see those on the wall. After all, good old great-grandfather Burnside owned whaling ships. That's where the money came from."

"As times are hard for some people and they scramble for cash, Scofield has been inundated with just such things."

"We'll not let go of ours," Louisa said staunchly.

The seamstress came back cradling the second black outfit and Caroline cooed over the velvet fabric. Again, they needed to help her into it, except this design had a swooping drape at the back.

Louisa turned Caroline so she could see all views. "And, you can pull the draping at the back and make it a hood, too. What do you think?"

"How clever! I like the stark look of the front and then the surprise of the back view." She pulled the back fabric up to frame her face.

"Just so," Louisa said, nodding.

They helped her out of the dress while the seamstress took it away and waited for her return, Caroline sat down and lit up a cigarette.

"You'd be surprised at some of the things people bring in thinking they are of value, only to be told that is not the case. Scofield works with several expert appraisers, and they, of course, have to verify the provenance of the piece. Tracing ownership from one person to another. In some cases, the piece has been in the public eye for generations and there is no doubt. Other cases are a bit more dodgy."

The seamstress came out with the red dress made of wool jersey designed to cling to the body. Caroline sighed and they got her into the dress.

"I hope you have someone at home to help you into these," Louisa said.

"Of course. José's family brought a raft of servants with them when they fled. My poor mother has had to take them all on and, of course, she doesn't speak Spanish and they simply refuse to learn English. Somehow, things get done."

The fabric of the red dress was fitted at the front and swept into deep folds at the back and admiring herself in the mirror, Caroline smiled broadly. Just at that moment, Monsieur Josef came into the room, gasped dramatically at the vision in front of him.

"Señora Guzmán. You are a vision!"

"Yes, I rather think I agree with you," she said turning to admire herself from all angles. The fabric was fitted at the waist and hips but flared out toward the hem, so the dress flowed as she moved.

Monsieur Josef applauded. "Well done, Louisa. Well done." He kissed her on both cheeks and left the room. His protegee was thrilled with the compliment.

"I think it is perfect as is," Caroline said.

They helped her out of the dress and into the robe again so she could sit down for a few minutes, light up another cigarette and recover from her exertions.

"A big night at the gallery Friday with a showing of new artists. If Scofield can stop fretting about that painting that he's trying to sell."

"What's that?"

"I don't know if you know the Warrens, but they're trying to liquidate some possessions and chose to part with a Turner, of all things. They've produced all kinds of evidence to authenticate it, but Scofield has a good eye and a better nose, and he senses something is not right."

Scofield? Hadn't Louisa heard Amanda and her father mentioning something about the art dealer?

Chapter 14

Brendan was parked outside her house waiting for the Warrens to drop Amanda off and waved hello to them before helping her with the luggage and the boxes.

"You packed a lot for such a short visit," he said, leaning over and kissing her.

"What will the neighbors say?" Amanda teased.

"They'll say I'm a lucky man." He had his arms full and pretended to stagger up the steps from the weight.

"Here, I've got a key," she said, not wanting to ring the bell and disrupt the maids, who had plenty to do preparing for the family's Christmas party. There was already a wreath on the door as they always timed the party for mid-month rather than the week of Christmas when there was so much competition with recitals, holiday performances, office gatherings and other families' events.

She held the vestibule door open as he went in and placed everything on the floor.

"Shall I take Madame's bags up to her room?"

She laughed. "Let's get some coffee. It's been a long drive. You've seen the newspapers, haven't you?"

"Of course. It's been all over the radio all day, too."

"Well, Rob Worley will be happy."

"I don't know how his business could be any better."

They went into the kitchen and Amanda was surprised that Cook was not there.

"Probably out getting provisions," she said.

"I thought you had them delivered," he said, which was not a usual practice in his parents' home.

"Yes, but I'm sure there is some special item or spice that will make or break the perfection of a particular dish. And she probably needed to get out of the house. Just look at all this!"

The countertops were laden with platters and serving dishes, a punch bowl and cups and seemingly most of the dishes and glasses in the house.

"You remember how to make coffee?" he asked her, thinking of her fumbling around the last time she offered.

"Yes," was her pointed answer. "It's not alchemy. Just water and the brown stuff in the can," she said, rummaging in a cabinet.

Brendan sat at the large butcher block table and watched her. "The Chief has called for all hands on deck for 'opening night,' as he called it. I think the term Bacchanal might be a more appropriate term."

"It's a good thing our party is the night after. The thought of all the rabble-rousing and inebriated drivers on the streets at the same time might keep our guests at home."

"I'm sure it's going to be a wild and wooly night. But probably not in this part of town."

Amanda had filled the pot, loaded the coffee into the basket and then lit the front burner on the range and put the coffee pot on. "See, not so hard. Now the one thing I don't know is how long I let it percolate before turning off the heat. Does longer mean stronger?"

"No, when it comes to a full boil, turn the heat down a little and let it perk for about three minutes. If it boils too hard or too long, it will be bitter."

"Oh, I had no idea."

"Well, living the bachelor life as I have for a bit, it is perhaps the only thing I can cook."

"Do you have to eat all your meals out, then?"

"Lunch, of course, and dinners with you. I also manage to mooch something from my family since they're only too happy to see me."

"If it's all hands on deck tomorrow night, are they expecting you to be out on the street with the possible bedlam going on?" Amanda hadn't considered the danger he might be in before that moment.

"The detectives will keep to their usual jobs, but there might be more incidents. Or we might be called in for back-up. There it goes," he said, referring to the water boiling and the water fountaining up through the glass cylinder on top of the lid. "Turn the heat down a bit. Let's time it." He glanced up at the clock on the wall.

"There's something I wanted to ask you about," he said. "There is the Annual Policeman's Ball on December twenty-third and I'm hoping you can come with me."

"That sounds like fun. Dressy?"

"Evening wear, absolutely. It's the one day that I don't recognize my colleagues. All cleaned up with impeccable manners."

The swinging door of the kitchen opened and Louisa came in with her portfolio tucked under her arm. "I thought I smelled coffee! Did you make it, Amanda?"

"Yes," her sister said. "I am capable of some things." She glanced at the clock and turned off the burner.

"Hello, Brendan. Have you heard about the end of the dreaded Prohibition?"

"I may look like it, but I don't live under a rock."

"Rob is preparing for a stellar evening. He's installed a fountain where the wine will pour out of the mouths of fish. Not real ones, of course. Doesn't that sound like fun?"

"I'm guessing you'd like some coffee, too?" Amanda asked.

"How kind of you," Louisa responded, taking her coat off. "Let me put these things away first," she said, leaving to do so.

Amanda got cups and saucers, cream and sugar, set them on the butcher block table and poured the coffee. "Smells like the real thing, don't you think?" she asked Brendan.

"Yes, indeed. You're a genius." He got up to give her a kiss as Louisa came back in.

"You'd better behave yourselves," she said.

Amanda rolled her eyes.

"Why, you really do know how to cook," Louisa said to her sister.

"This is the first thing I've ever made, and it was pretty simple. I wouldn't call it cooking."

"You better make sure that there is enough in that trust fund of yours so you can afford a cook or you're going to starve." Louisa looked back and forth at them.

"I'm not going anywhere just yet, dear," Amanda said sharply.

The back door opened and Cook bustled in with a paper grocery bag in her hand. She stopped short at the sight of the occupied kitchen.

"Did Mary or Simona do that?" she asked, putting the bag down on the counter.

"No. I did it. Would you like a cup of coffee?"

This was an uncomfortable moment for Cook, who made all the meals but never took one with the family and certainly not afternoon coffee in her own kitchen. The young women sensed her unease.

"We'd better leave Cook to her kingdom. Lots to do before the party," Amanda said, taking her cup and saucer out to the dining room as Louisa and Brendan followed.

"How was your short visit to the Cape?" Louisa asked when they were seated.

"Sad and dramatic. The house felt so empty and as I walked around trying to match my memories with the current state of the place, it was odd what I remembered and what I didn't."

"You were in grade school. I'm surprised you could recall anything."

"There was this painting in a prominent place in the study and evidently it is gone. At least, I think it must be. There is the slightly lighter rectangle on the wall where something used to hang and that lent to the atmosphere of loss. Not just because something was gone, but because I couldn't remember what was there in the first place. And then Kitty's uncle was absolutely horrid. Burst into the house and acted brutish."

"Why?" Louisa asked.

"First, he accused Mrs. Warren of trying to make off with the family's things when she told him she was only trying to retrieve her own possessions." She left out the part about the doctor and the sheriff coming by, knowing that Louisa might blab about it and was saving that information for Brendan, who might make some sense of it. "Then, a local lawyer popped in to let her know about some land dispute and told her that her husband had changed his will and she was to inherit the house."

"As his wife, why shouldn't she?" Brendan asked.

"There was some assumption that his brother would get the house," Amanda said.

"Is such a will valid?" Louisa asked.

"If it was done in the same state—and the last time I checked, Hyannis is in Massachusetts—and if properly witnessed and executed, yes, it is valid."

"Even so, he stormed about and said he would contest it. Naturally, Mrs. Warren did not want to stay there much longer, especially since she wanted to verify the validity of the new will with her Boston attorney. I was more than happy to leave, as well."

"Sounds like a mess," Louisa said.

"And Mrs. Warren is going back down soon not to pack up but probably to inventory what is there. I wouldn't be surprised if August shows up to claim that something or other was promised to him by their father or some such nonsense."

"Death in the family can sometimes bring out the worst in people," Brendan commented.

"How has Mr. Barlow allowed you to be away? I thought you were working on another project for him," Louisa said.

"I think you must have been daydreaming through most of the conversations around the dinner table. Mr. Barlow is leaving the hospital; he offered me a job, which I have declined, and I don't know how things stand. In fact, I should probably call in to make an appointment for tomorrow to discuss things with Mrs. Tyrell, Chair of the Board of Directors," Amanda said.

Brendan looked at his watch. "I have to be going soon, but it's early enough in the day for you to make the call, don't you think?"

"Good idea." Amanda got up and went to her father's study and called the hospital administration offices from there. Miss Bailey answered the call.

"Hello, Miss Burnside," she said in the sort of tone that suggested she was not alone in the Director's outer office.

"May I speak to Mr. Barlow?"

"I'm sorry, Mr. Barlow is no longer with Mercy Hospital."

Amanda was floored but quickly recovered. "Has anyone else taken his place?"

"Not at this time," Miss Bailey said. The she added, "Good afternoon" to someone who gave her the same greeting in response. The ding of the elevator sounded in the background and a few moments passed before she resumed. "Mr. Barlow was planning on leaving at the end of the week but there's been a huge ruckus. Mrs. Tyrell was furious that he felt he needed to go and on such short notice and called an emergency meeting of the Board and, of course, I was there taking minutes." She lowered her voice. "On the agenda was the removal of Mrs. Tyrell as Board Chair and the vote was unanimous. Except she voted nay."

"What? I thought she was doing a wonderful job."

"Mr. Hegeman nominated Mr. Larsen, who wanted the Chair position all along, and he was voted in by a majority. And then Mrs. Tyrell resigned and walked out of the room in tears."

"That's awful."

"Mr. Larsen said that the hospital's budget was getting out of control with all the additional programs that Mr. Barlow had put in place."

"Like the clinics," Amanda said with resignation.

"He wasn't specific at the meeting. But to save money, he suggested that he take over the Director's job in addition to being the Board Chair until things were stabilized. Then they could seek a replacement."

"So, the hospital is back to the same organizational scheme that it was when a physician was the Director and Board Chair. Ugh."

"Miss Burnside, I'm sorry to tell you that he had me type up a letter requesting your resignation today."

That hit Amanda like a punch in the stomach. All she could muster was, "I'm not surprised. The man never liked me much and as soon as the hospital stops spending money on free clinics, the bottom line ought to recover."

"I'm so sorry. I thought it was a marvelous program."

"Me, too!" Amanda said staunchly. "And I'd do it again if given the opportunity.'

They were silent a few moments.

"I have a few personal things still there—perhaps an umbrella and a calendar."

"They're still in your office. Oh, I'll miss you," Miss Bailey said. "Things won't be the same."

"Things are never the same. Ever changing. We have to adjust. I'll stop by in the next few days and pick up my things. Take care, now," Amanda said and hung up.

She knew she ought to be sad or upset, but she was angry at the way everything had been done. Had they called the Board meeting when she was gone on purpose? It just seemed so scheming and underhanded. Poor Mrs. Tyrell, who was one of the hardest-working members of the Board. They might well be sorry when they realized how much money she had donated over the years, funds that might find a home in a different charity that would appreciate her dedication.

Amanda reappeared in the dining room and announced, "I'm free! They've booted me out. I no longer have a job."

"I'm so sorry," Brendan said with concern when she sat down.

"How can they do that?" Louisa asked.

"They want to save money. As if I was costing them anything significant." She took a sip of cold coffee from the cup in front of her. "The clinics were costing them staff time and how stupid in these times, when people really need it, that they decide to cut a vital program. Well, obviously they didn't like Mr. Barlow. They felt threatened by his modern notions. Good riddance."

"What are you going to do now?"

"Eat bonbons and read fashion magazines, of course," Amanda said.

That got a laugh out of Brendan who put his hand over hers. "You'll land on your feet."

∽

THE LANDING WAS SOONER and softer than she expected. When she broke the news in the sitting room prior to dinner, her parents were dismayed.

"That's terrible. And what a shabby way to let you know that your efforts were not appreciated," her mother said stoutly.

Her father shook his head. "The way of the world. Politics in the boardroom, politics everywhere."

"Which party?" Mrs. Burnside asked, misconstruing his comment.

"I meant individual politics of who gets to be in charge and why. And stupidly, it is often down to personality conflict, not real disagreement."

"In this case, I think it was a bit of both," Amanda said. "Mr. Barlow was a youngish, forward-thinking person and most of the Board are—old sticks. Set in their ways, 'let's not try something new, we don't want to spend too much money, 'those people are poor because they're lazy' kind of thinking." She looked at her mother's shocked face. "Really, I overheard one of them asking why they were giving away such good care, as if poor people should get a substandard level of health care. Can you imagine?"

"I'm afraid I can. America was built on the notion that all you have to do is work hard and you'll succeed. Of course, that's nonsense. Plenty of people work hard and don't have much to show for it. And plenty of others don't work at all, have it easy and feel their position is entitled."

Amanda knew her father was more progressive in his thinking than he let on—not that he had voted for Roosevelt—but he had never expressed himself so clearly.

At that moment, where his family was almost open-mouthed after that screed, Mary appeared and announced that dinner was ready. As they walked into the dining room, he pulled on Amanda's arm.

"In the meantime, until you find your feet, why don't you keep working on Gilbert's files?"

"I'd be happy to do that. I took them with me to Hyannis but didn't get a chance to look at a single one. A lot of Warren family drama there, and I'll tell you after dinner if you're interested. I'll go to your office tomorrow after I pick up my things from the hospital."

He patted her on the arm. "I think we might be able to pay you as a part-time employee."

"Really? That would be nice."

"But that divorce case…." He looked uncomfortable.

"If you want me to take on Gilbert's cases, then I will take on all of them including those folders from Mr. Van Eaton. I can at least write up a summary from the notes Gilbert created."

"And have young Van Eaton review them. His secretary can type them up and he'll decide what to do next."

"Divorce has become more common, and we don't need to be coy about the details," she said.

He raised his eyebrows as if not entirely sure he agreed with her position.

She hooked her arm in his. "This will be interesting and fun. You know I love solving puzzles and mysteries."

The divorce case was simple compared to how tangled all the issues were with the Warrens. And not as much fun as she anticipated.

Chapter 15

The next day, Amanda dressed in one of her smartest suits and drove to Mercy Hospital to pick up what few personal possessions she had left there. With her head held high, she went to the administrative floor and was greeted by the mournful face of Miss Bailey.

"Good morning," Amanda said cheerfully. "Don't look so downcast. I've already got another job."

"Have you?" The young secretary was beaming. Looking over Miss Bailey's shoulder she saw that Mr. Larsen hadn't come in yet, which was just as well as far as she was concerned.

"I'll just go to my office—my *former* office—and pick up my things," Amanda said, not feeling as happy as she had presented herself. Her desk was as neat as she had left it, with folders in a standing metal rack, each filled with paperwork relating to the three clinics she had helped organize. What a shame if they were to be discontinued. She looked through the drawers of the desk, pushing paper clips aside to retrieve a nickel that had somehow found its way there. Index cards were in the top right-hand drawer and since she had purchased them, they were going into her purse. A pair of driving gloves that she had forgotten about were in one of the lower drawers. And then there was her engagement book that she flipped through, with all the notes, names, addresses and telephone numbers of people she had worked with over the past months. A wistful smile came to her face. Whatever the current Board thought, she had done a darned good job, learned a lot about different neighborhoods and ethnic groups, how organizations worked and, yes, helped the community. She felt proud.

She took her umbrella from the coatrack in the corner, noticing that the desk Valerie had once worked at still had no occupant. "Oh, well. Not my business." She walked back out to the reception desk.

"Here is the letter that Mr. Larsen had me type up. I guess we can save a stamp if I give it to you." Miss Bailey handed it to her.

"Yes, we must economize!" She looked at it and back at Miss Bailey. "Should I just tear it up?"

"I wouldn't do that. The letter is short and bland, but your last paycheck is in there, too."

"Smart thinking." She held out her hand to the secretary. "Goodbye. Thank you for all your help. And good luck with the new administration. You have my home number if you need anything."

"Like a reference?" Miss Bailey asked, taking her hand and shaking it.

"I'd be happy to provide one. Let me get out of here before I run into anyone I know."

Amanda got into the elevator, smiled and waved but still felt that lump in her throat as she had at her graduation. A deep breath and she went all the way to the ground floor without interruption and sailed out the door to her car.

Her father must have told the other partners and the front office staff about Amanda's assignment because they all greeted her by name and one receptionist was even kind enough to escort her to Gilbert's office. The two boxes that she had dragged to Hyannis sat on top of the desk.

Taking off her coat, hat and gloves, she put her umbrella on the hook behind the door and surveyed the desk's contents again. Now that she was going to be spending some time here, she thought about a quick inventory of what she might need. Good thing she brought the index cards and her engagement calendar with her. The phone rang and she stared at it. It rang again and she picked it up gingerly.

"Good morning, Miss Burnside," her father said.

"Good morning to you again, Mr. Burnside. Thank you for bringing those boxes in. I only remembered that I left them at home when I entered the building. But I must ask you, is anyone here upset or curious that your daughter is now an employee?"

"You mean nepotism? Don't be ridiculous. Nepotism is only a bad thing when the unqualified are put in positions that they can't manage. Most of the staff here were hired because of some relationship to existing employees. In certain types of business, that's a good thing as there is a sense of allegiance that someone off the street might not have. And after all, we are a family law firm. Had you been a boy, I'm sure I would have expected you to attend college and law school and come in with me."

There it was again. "You know, Daddy, I have come to regret not going to college. It's probably too late to do so, but law school? I don't know."

"Water under the bridge. You're doing fine. Let me know if you need anything. Let Esther know if you need supplies of any kind. Welcome aboard."

The desk was dusty, likewise the bureau behind the desk and sliding the bottom doors open, she was shocked to find more stacks of files. She closed them quickly and realized she had nothing to clean things off with so went out to the front desk to seek Esther, who seemed embarrassed that no one had cleaned or dusted Gilbert's office.

"I'm sorry, Miss Burnside. He was particular about people going into his office. Everyone here handles confidential information, but he seemed to take his privacy or secrecy to another level. I'll get a dust cloth."

Amanda was about to protest before she realized that she was not expected to clean or empty her own ashtray—if she smoked—and someone surely came in and vacuumed and washed the one window in the little room she occupied. The dusting was completed quickly, and Esther smiled and left Amanda to once again sort through the files and make notes about whom she needed to talk to or follow up with. The divorce case files had been returned and she decided to leave them for another day. After her trip to Hyannis and the discussion about the painting, not to mention Louisa's second-hand connection with the Scofield Gallery, that was the file she wanted to look at first.

The client was the gallery owner, who had suspicions about the provenance of the Warren painting that he had agreed to sell for a commission. In looking through the paperwork, Amanda came across a photo of the painting and, in seeing it, smiled when it brought back a vague memory of seeing it on the wall at Belvedere. There were several close-up shots of the artist's signature and one of the back of the painting, which she thought was odd because she realized she had never looked at the back of any painting. This one showed the canvas stretched across a wooden frame with additional signatures affixed on paper labels or the wood itself.

Flipping through the pages looking for more photographs, she came across the one again of the woman in a flamboyant Edwardian paisley gown, pearls, many bracelets and a period hairstyle. Behind her was the painting hanging in the place it had always been in the house although the furniture was different. Turning it over there was a date on it and 'B. Warren.'

A grandparent? Or great-grandparent? She looked back to the front and smiled at the figure who must have been at the height of artistic fashion at the time, practically a bohemian, yet to modern eyes looked just like every other older woman of the time. Stiff—probably in a corset—strange piled-up hair, yet she had an attitude of defiance. Just as our descendants will look at pictures of us, she thought, laughing at our ridiculous styles.

Back to the paperwork, though. The original request had come from Scofield, who, according to the notes that the attorney had made, typed up and carbon copied to the investigator, had some hesitation about accepting the painting. He knew it to be extremely rare and valuable and, while it might not entice a younger collector unless as an investment, it would be an important acquisition to a long-time Bostonian or a newcomer who sought social acceptance, or even a well-funded museum. It looked like there had been months of negotiations that began with the Warren brothers and Scofield, mainly about what was an appropriate asking price but most of all, what commission the gallerist would charge. Then the interactions fell to August to continue since Rupert had other business interests on his mind. They agreed on a final asking price, which made Amanda's eyebrows go up, and

Scofield had capitulated to a lower commission than he wanted. He still believed in the authenticity of the painting, but something about August nagged at him.

Amanda wondered what it was that Scofield expected the law firm to do except hold his hand and tell him everything was all right. Perhaps the best thing to do was to talk with the attorney assigned to the case and then Scofield himself. She was unsure of the firm's protocols—did she need to make an appointment with the lawyer's secretary, or could she just pop in to ask him a few questions? Instead, she went to her father and asked how to approach it.

"Secretary, first. Most people like to get notice of an impending meeting to prepare for it."

"There's no preparation needed. I just wanted to ask him for his opinion of the gallery owner's intentions."

"It's not a matter of paperwork, it has to do with being mentally prepared. He has only met you once in some social situation and now you're wearing a different hat, so to speak. We all learn to think quickly on our feet, but it's a courtesy to let him know the general topic ahead of time. And he is one of the senior partners."

"I'm glad I asked you," Amanda said.

Amanda showed up outside the man's office where the secretary motioned her to sit down while she used the intercom to announce the arrival. Then, with great ceremony, she was ushered into Mr. Wheeler's spacious office. He stood up and gestured to a chair opposite his desk, which had one folder on it, resumed his seat and beamed at her.

"Well, Burnside's daughter. I think it's been years since I last saw you."

"I think you're right."

"You young people grow up so quickly," he said, looking down at the folder, signaling that he was ready for business.

Amanda took a quick look around while his head was down to see how he had decorated his office, which she always felt was indicative of an individual's personality. His was austere with dark wood furniture, several diplomas and plaques on the wall and behind him a framed photograph of a woman with grey hair. One wall held a bookcase with the requisite law books that formed the cornerstone of legal décor, but there were no golf clubs in the corner or photos of sailboats, horses or dogs. All business.

"I understand our man Gilbert has left us rather abruptly," he said, looking up.

"My father said there were health issues and he had to go to a drier climate."

He smiled without showing teeth, raised his eyebrows and pretended to be reading the cover sheet of the file for the first time. "What was the status of his investigation?"

"I was hoping you could tell me. There are notes of all kinds," she said, opening the file on her lap. "Photos, too, and a report from some appraiser."

"I'll be frank with you, Miss Burnside. It seemed to me that Mr. Scofield didn't have any specific issue with the impending sale. It had more to do with his confidence—or lack thereof—in the sellers."

"The Warrens?"

"They suffered after the Crash, as many people have, so selling a valuable asset made sense from their point of view. That wasn't the problem. It was August Warren who made Mr. Scofield uncomfortable."

Amanda was about to let him know she might see why but decided not to interject her opinion at that time.

"August Warren's reputation has been tarnished over the years by, shall we say, his involvement with certain people and financial schemes that were technically legal but not entirely above board. His brother, Rupert, was the co-owner of the painting, which gave Mr. Scofield some comfort, but as the negotiations continued—and Mr. Gilbert was not privy to those conversations—he became increasingly uncomfortable. August Warren pressed him harder and kept visiting the gallery."

"It sounds as if he were desperate."

"I believe he was. Rupert not so much. The more August pushed, the more skittish Mr. Scofield became. A specialist from New York came up and examined it extensively along with the paperwork and some photos and declared it legitimate. So, for all intents and purposes, the investigation is closed in my mind."

"Oh," Amanda said. "That's a relief. It's one less thing for me to follow up on."

"And I spoke to Mr. Scofield just last week and he has been in possession of the painting for some time and will be showing it in his usual gallery evenings."

"I'm sorry, when are those?"

"It seems he has a soiree every other week, usually Thursday, where he invites his clientele as well as the public to come in, have some canapes, a glass of champagne—all legal now, you know—and browse. When possible, the artist himself is present, although in the case of the Warrens' piece, that's not possible, since the artist left us many years ago."

Amanda put her head down so he wouldn't see her smile at his flowery prose.

"So, all is well?"

"It would seem so. It is a magnificent painting, and I'm sure he'll find a buyer."

Amanda smiled. "After all this, I have a mind to take a look at the painting that I haven't seen in many years."

"You do that now. Case closed as far as I'm concerned." He smiled again and stood, indicating the meeting was over. They shook hands and Amanda left, more curious than ever to see what all the fuss had been about. Was this Boston's answer to the Mona Lisa?

She went back to her office, put on her hat, coat and gloves and walked to the Scofield Gallery, which was only about fifteen blocks away. It was cold but the smidgen of sun made it a pleasant winter walk since she kept in the lee of the buildings; it was only when she came to a crosswalk that she was hit with the full force of the wind.

As she left the commercial district of banks, law firms and businesses, she came to the upscale shops of couturier clothing, antiques, home furnishings and galleries. These had sprung up close to the business sector in the expectation that the after-work pedestrian traffic would bring the right sort of customer. At that time of day, still early afternoon, however, there were few people on the street, and she wondered if the gallery would even be open.

There was no open/closed sign on the inside of the glass door, but Scofield might have considered that too tacky. She tried the door and found it locked. Amanda knocked on the door and someone came out from the back, smiled at her and unlocked the door. To her surprise, it was Caroline Browne, now Guzmán.

"Oh, hello. I knew you worked here but somehow didn't expect to see you.

"Come in, it's cold."

Amanda noticed that Caroline had on an unusual outfit in black jersey with strange sleeves and wore heavy earrings and a necklace of large, polished stones. It was quite unlike anything she had seen her wear before but then she had only seen her in social situations and at the Oasis. This outfit was totally appropriate for an art gallery but would look out of place at a nightclub.

"I'm glad you've come to see the gallery. Scofield will be so pleased. He's in the back now, but when he hears us talking, he'll come out. I'm just getting things ready for this evening. We're having an open gallery as he calls it. Our usual customers and the press have been invited, although to be honest, the press is fairly ignorant about art of any kind. They are more interested in the hors d'oeuvres—you'd think they didn't have enough to eat." She laughed.

"From my experience, they don't get paid much so a free drink and food is much appreciated. I certainly hope they give you a good write-up in return."

"They do and the beauty of it is that, because they don't have a clue about art, we can spoon-feed them information and you can see it in the write-up the next day in the paper almost word for word." She laughed again.

"You used to have a gallery in New York, isn't that right?"

"Yes, I loved it. *Très moderne* and ahead of its time. My clients were collectors, not decorators looking for something that would complement the carpeting or the furniture. A select group and they, like many others, suffered after the stock market fell. Business dropped and it was wisest to close. And

José was tired of Manhattan if you can imagine. It broke my heart, but life goes on."

Amanda wondered how someone like the sophisticated José could have become tired of the bustle and excitement of New York. Unless something else persuaded him to leave. "You seem to be happy now, and that's important. I came to see the gallery but really wanted to look at the Warren painting. I know the family but haven't seen it for years."

"It's in the back in a position of great honor. For such an old piece, it looks so modern."

They passed plinths with sculptures on them and walls lined with paintings since the premises, although narrow, extended far back to the alley.

"So that's the Turner." Amanda said.

"Good marks for you," said a voice from the back of the gallery.

Amanda turned to see a slim man in a tight-fitting suit and white shirt set off at the neck with an ascot. His urbane look was accented with a pencil moustache.

Caroline made the introductions.

"Burnside? I recognize the name from the law firm."

Amanda smiled but did not let on that she knew his name in that connection as well.

She looked back to the painting. The photographs she had seen didn't do it justice.

"Yes. The Warrens wanted me to buy it outright. That was before they found out how much it was worth. No gallery owner—not even me—could afford it. Or should I say, would be willing to lay out the asking price and wait a few years for it to sell."

Amanda turned her head away from the nautical scene. "That's not what Kitty's uncle said. He made it sound as if it would go quickly."

Scofield shook his head with disdain. "That may be what he said, but I have repeatedly tried to disabuse him of that notion. Even something as special as this will take time. Art is a long game, after all."

"Well, it's quite beautiful," Amanda said, continuing to gaze at the misty clouds and the half-light behind the sails of the ship. But she was still puzzled at August's expectations and wondered what that meant for the family finances.

Chapter 16

As Amanda was coming in the front door of her house, Louisa was on her way out.

"Oh, could you give me a lift downtown?" she asked.

Amanda's shoulders sagged at the thought of making the return trip. "A bit early for the Oasis, isn't it?"

"I'm on my way to the gallery. I'm dying to see Caroline in my creation. And I'd like to get a glimpse of what the art scene is like."

"I saw her and the creation, as you termed it, and it looks wonderful. There, you don't have to go now."

Louisa made a hurt face. "It won't take long."

"I hope you're not thinking of changing first."

Louisa's wistful look indicated that she had considered changing her clothes, restyling her hair and touching up her makeup. The sensible thing to do would be for Amanda to lend her car to her sister, but that presented the temptation of her staying out till all hours. They had a short standoff.

"I could...."

"It's either now or never," Amanda said, turning around and going back to the garage. "I was just there, as a matter of fact." Her sister trotted to catch up to her.

"You'll have a ride back?"

"I might take a taxi."

They drove in silence, with most of the traffic going the other way.

"If you promise to only be ten minutes or so, I could wait outside."

"Thank you, that would be wonderful."

Amanda's thought of waiting outside was dispelled by parked cars on both sides of the street. It meant a good turnout for the gallery but no place to wait in her auto.

"Look, someone is pulling out ahead," Louisa said, and Amanda signaled and pulled her car into the spot.

"Ten minutes, right?" Amanda confirmed.

She could have kept the engine and the heater running but that seemed like a waste of gasoline, so she turned it off. In the backseat of the car was yesterday's newspaper, which she had already read but decided to work on the crossword puzzle while she waited. There was a sinking feeling that she'd be there more than ten minutes although she lost track of time watching the steady influx of patrons.

Louisa was pleased by the turnout and, scanning the crowd, saw that there were as many women as men present. Why hadn't she thought to get business cards made up? That would be her next step. Louisa Burnside, Couturier. Or Designer? Or Louisa's Designs? She was still dressed in day clothes and noticed that many of the women were, as well, although a few had ventured into somber evening wear. Caroline was several feet inside the front door, greeting people by name and having them sign a book. She caught Louisa's eye.

"Well?" Caroline mouthed, turning to the side to show off one of the new creations.

When it was Louisa's turn to write her name and address in the book, she said, "You look fantastic, if I do say so. What did Scofield say?"

"He nodded his approval. That's high praise from him. I've got to welcome the guests, but why don't you go over and introduce yourself? Be prepared for him to be preoccupied, however."

"I'll make it quick," Louisa said and went over to the only man in the room who could be Scofield. He was by turns smiling, suppressing a scowl at something not going right and then lighting up at the approach of a well-heeled guest. Louisa stood behind a middle-aged couple who said their hellos and made a few comments before moving off. She stepped up and saw that he gave her a once-over, judging her appearance and age and concluding that she probably couldn't afford anything he was exhibiting.

Nonetheless, Louisa held out her hand and introduced herself and explained that she had designed Caroline's outfit for the night.

His stiff smile behind the pencil moustache widened into something more genuine. "She looks lovely. I see you have talent," he said. He adjusted his ascot, and the sudden thought came to her that perhaps she would make him one in some interesting silk pattern. Just because.

"I just stopped in to see the gallery; I've never been in here before. I see that you have a good turnout."

Amanda was struggling with the crossword puzzle in the meager interior light of her car, and she was starting to get cold. She got out, locked the car, and decided to walk up and down the sidewalk until Louisa came out. An interior design shop two doors down featured a miniature living room with mirrors, glass and metal just like she had seen in some movie recently. She peered through the windows of the closed shop and saw sleek, modern white furniture that would look ridiculous in their sitting room. On further thought, since this was the future of design, how could they ever adapt the Beacon Hill house to accommodate such styles without removing all traces of wood, knocking down walls and totally changing the place? It wasn't going to happen in her lifetime.

She looked at her watch and then at the entrance to the gallery and saw her sister coming out onto the pavement, looking for her. Louisa was almost knocked down by a large man, who removed his hat to apologize.

It was August Warren. What was he doing here? Of course, he wanted to see what kind of traffic the gallery brought in and by the turnout, he ought to have been pleased. Perhaps he also wanted to stand by the painting, thinking that his presence and ownership would give some cachet to the Turner, which could stand on its own merits.

August stepped around Louisa and into the vestibule and when she turned, she saw Amanda waving at her.

"I can't believe it—you really were only ten minutes. That man who almost ran you down was Kitty's Uncle August."

Louisa turned to look. "I didn't get a very good look at him."

"He and Kitty's father looked alike. There are all kinds of difficulties going on after he died, however."

They got into the car and quickly exited the parking space as someone else was waiting to take it.

"The uncle ended up not getting the Hyannis house and he is not pleased. I think he is eager to have the painting sell but he'll have to split the money with Mrs. Warren."

"Caroline said it is a museum-quality piece. But she also said sometimes it takes years for such things to sell," Louisa said.

"I know Mrs. Warren wants to keep the house on the Cape, but keeping up two homes without her husband's income might be impossible," Amanda said.

"Gosh, I've never given it much thought. One incident and everything could turn around in an instant. We've got to take good care of Daddy."

Chapter 17

December was a month full of celebrations and the night following the gallery opening was the Burnsides' open house. That type of party wasn't a new concept but had become more popular in recent years because people could drop in during a certain period, share holiday cheer, have a bite to eat and then move on to the next venue. Mrs. Burnside hosted one every year and it was less nerve-racking than a sit-down dinner for a dozen people. That didn't mean she was in any less of a state because of the casual mode of entertaining. On the contrary, she seemed to worry more not knowing how many people would show up, if they would come in a steady stream or in overwhelming waves and, ridiculously, whether she would have enough food. Every year, during the first ten minutes of the appointed start time, she panicked, thinking the invitations hadn't gone out, although she had received the requisite responses; that the weather would prevent people from going out, although the weather was as it always was in December and no Arctic storm ever occurred; and that somehow another, more enticing invitation had come to the mailboxes of her friends and social circle, although there was no rival when it came to her hospitality.

Amanda and Louisa stayed home the day of the party although they didn't know if they were of any help to their mother or were of more use getting out of the way. Their presence seemed to befuddle her when she was in the midst of giving instructions to the maids about the layout of the plates and glasses despite Mary having done this task many times before. Simona, who was newer to the task, thought that arranging them was self-evident and couldn't understand Mrs. Burnside's distress.

Not only was the dining room layout the same as always, with some chairs lined against the wall and others moved into the sitting room, the décor was the same from year to year— with garlands over the fireplaces, the Christmas tree in one corner, a floral arrangement on a table and poinsettias adding seasonal color. Even the menu was the same from year to year with a ham, hors d'oeuvres, and Cook's Christmas cookies and fruitcake. They always served eggnog, and this year there was another mildly alcoholic punch since the President had signed the authorization to end Prohibition that very day.

The sisters went out for a late lunch, not daring to impose on Cook or get in the way of the preparations. They chose a tearoom close to downtown where women often stopped after a day of shopping.

"You know Mother could just as easily have this party catered each year. I'm sure it wouldn't cost any more than what we already spend. They even bring in the plates and glasses and take it all away when it's over," Louisa said, looking at the menu.

"There would be a rebellion from Cook as much as she grumbles and groans in anticipation of and during the event. And she would criticize everything from the food to the presentation. There would be no living with her."

"Here's a better idea. We give her a two-day vacation while the party goes on. How can she not appreciate that?

Amanda laughed. "I would bet you she'd sneak in just to see what was going on and wonder what they were doing to *her* kitchen."

"You're right. I'll have the soup and bread," Louisa said to the waitress and Amanda ordered the same.

"Is Rob having his celebratory opening tonight?" Amanda asked.

"Yes, and the timing is excellent in that there will be so many people wandering around our house that nobody will notice I'm gone."

"At one o'clock in the morning, they certainly will. And don't try the pillows under the blankets made to look like a sleeping body trick. They're on to that."

"I thought I would just go out and if they ask, you'll tell them where I am."

Amanda shot her a look. "How about if you leave a note and I will hand it to them and act just as surprised as they are when they read it?"

"I rather like that idea. If there is a note, they may jump to the conclusion that I've eloped and be immensely relieved to find out that I've only gone out to another party. You're brilliant.

Is Brendan coming tonight?"

"Yes, although I hope he doesn't find it too stuffy."

"What? Our parents' friends stuffy?" Louisa giggled. "Can't you just imagine Doctor Osborne with a lampshade on his head?"

Amanda laughed. "Thank you for that image. Now that's all I'll think of when I see him."

They chatted amiably through lunch, each periodically checking a wristwatch as they counted down the minutes and hours until the famed annual family holiday party.

Less than five hours later, the Burnsides were stationed in the sitting room awaiting the first of their guests. Right on schedule, the Fosters, who always arrived either first or early, appeared at the door, carefully holding a bottle of alcohol wrapped in paper.

"Merry Christmas and Happy End of Prohibition!" Mr. Foster declared.

Mary took their coats while further greetings were exchanged, and they were taken into the dining room by Louisa, who offered them drinks. The doorbell rang again and so it went for the first thirty minutes as the rooms filled with chattering people, some already helping themselves to the enormous spread of food. At last, Brendan arrived, his blue eyes sharply picking Amanda out of the crowd before handing his overcoat to Simona and walking across the room. Most of the men were dressed in suits but Brendan had worn his evening clothes, the black material showing off his dark hair and eyelashes. He took Amanda's hands and kissed her on the cheek.

"Are you having a wonderful time?" he asked her.

"I am now. Come, let me get you a drink and introduce you to some of our friends." More of the party was taking place in the dining room where people stood with drinks in hand or a plate of food. Everyone noticed that Amanda had linked her arm in that of a handsome young man and some approached, to get acquainted.

"A policeman! Really," said Mrs. Portland, who lived next door. Her eyes were wide with interest.

"A detective, actually," he said.

"Head of the detectives," Amanda added.

"You must have had some exciting cases." She took him by the arm and pulled him away to ask him something in a whisper.

Amanda was left to herself and, glancing toward the door, saw that Fred Browne, her former boyfriend, and his fiancée Valerie had come in with his mother, Hextilda, flamboyantly dressed in a red brocade dress looking like a wrapped package under the tree. She made a beeline for Amanda, and they exchanged air kisses.

"Aren't you glowing? I think I see why, and if he were my beau, I wouldn't let him out of my sight." She nudged Amanda, who had lowered her head to mask her blush and annoyance.

"Will Caroline and José be coming?" Amanda asked.

"They're at the Oasis. Big grand re-opening tonight," she said, waving her hands in mock enthusiasm. "As if people haven't been drinking for the past however many years."

"At least they won't be getting rotgut," Fred said, coming closer. "You can't imagine how many cases we've had of alcohol poisoning."

Hextilda rolled her eyes at her son's inappropriately somber party chatter and went to survey the food. Amanda could not imagine her as a mother-in-law and silently wished Valerie the best of luck. At that moment, she felt enormous sympathy for her friend and took her by the arm and offered her some punch.

"How are things? How are the wedding plans coming along?"

"There is so much to do. I'm sorry I haven't been in to help at the hospital."

"Don't apologize. Mr. Barlow is gone—didn't Fred tell you? And with it the exciting job I had carved out for myself."

"Oh, that's sad! You were so good at it." Valerie's large brown eyes were close to tears.

Amanda patted her arm. "Life goes on. I'm helping my father with some things."

Valerie leaned in closer to whisper, "You've heard about Kitty's father?"

"Yes dreadful. I was down at the Cape helping her and her mother sort through some things."

"Who do they suspect? You always seem to know about these things."

"Since it happened in Hyannis, the sheriff there oversees the investigation. I've met him once."

"You have?" Valerie said with either fear or awe.

"He stopped by the house, that's all. Have you had some ham? My mother orders it specially from someplace in Virginia. I think she and my father honeymooned in Washington and they had it at some well-known restaurant and she managed to cadge the name of the vendor from the chef. So, every year...."

"That's a lovely story. Fred and I are talking about honeymoon locations. So many decisions. Where is Louisa?"

Amanda scanned the room and muttered, "Good question." Then more audibly, she said, "Excuse me, I do need to find her." She went into the sitting room, the study and, after exhausting all the public rooms, went upstairs and couldn't tell from looking in Louisa's room whether she had left or not. In her own room, she found her handbag open on her dresser. Unless one of their guests was a cat burglar, there was the more likely explanation that her sister had taken the keys to her car.

THE OASIS WAS THROBBING with the music of the band, whose singer couldn't be heard above the loud talking and laughter of the crowd and had given up, saving her voice. The night was still young, but the place had been packed since six o'clock with many people standing because seats were no longer available. Rob Worley was thrilled with the turnout and hoped that no one from the Fire Department would show up and make them adhere to the occupancy limit; he had gone to the trouble of inviting one of the Chiefs, who had readily accepted, to forestall any problems.

Louisa had left her family's annual party and it took her a good ten minutes to make her way through the crowd to where he stood, surveying the bustle. A good thing he had hired on six more waiters for the night as they were all being run off their feet.

"At last," he said, kissing her cheek. "And what do you think of our fountain?"

"What a success," she said. "I can't believe how many people are squashed in here. You're going to make a fortune tonight."

"Tonight and every night. And no more fear of police raids."

"Hear! Hear!"

"And what would my lady like to drink?"

"A martini would be lovely," Louisa said, smiling up at him.

"How is Monsieur Josef?"

"Loving my work, thank you. I suggested he come here tonight but he is under the impression that the entire town will be drunk and brawling on the streets, and he'll have no part of that. He's probably sitting in his apartment sipping a tisane."

"There'll be little brawling since the police have increased their presence, especially in this, the entertainment district."

"Is that what you're calling it these days?"

"Yes, and some of the other owners of legitimate clubs—well, I guess we're all legitimate now—are banding together to request that we have more police on view rather than less. We want patrons to know that they are safe. If tonight and the next few nights go smoothly, we'll approach the Mayor about it. Good idea, huh?" he said.

"Brilliant," Louisa agreed.

"There he is now," Rob said with his eyes on the entrance as the Mayor and his assistant stood surveying the scene before deciding to join the merriment by handing their overcoats to the hat-check girl. As befitted an honored guest, Rob wove through the crowd to greet them.

"This is going to be a great thing for Boston," the Mayor said as they shook hands warmly. "Just think of the revenue we'll get."

"And the police ought to be relieved of what has been an over-load of cases of bootlegging and violence," Rob said with a straight face as if he had been no part of the illegal activity himself.

"I'm afraid we won't be rid of the folks who want to evade the rules of the Alcoholic Beverages Control Commission. There will always be moonshiners," the Mayor said.

"Home brewing has gone on forever, but now that people know the liquor they are buying is safe to drink, you're right, there will be an uptick in revenue."

The Mayor looked around the room approvingly. "As long as things don't get out of hand."

BACK AT THE BURNSIDES' house, it was a more sedate bunch who mingled in small groups, avoiding the topics of politics and religion as they had been taught as children, but seeing as how they shared the same political and religious beliefs, it had been an unnecessary caution. It left the topics of the weather, family updates and who was going where for the holidays. Amanda could see that, after the initial revelation of Brendan's occupation, there was little fodder for conversation.

"How would you like to go to a concert?" he asked her.

"Now?"

"Yes. There is free admission."

"Really? Where is this?"

"It's at Angela and Sean's school," he said, referring to his younger siblings. "She's in the choir and he's in the orchestra. I should make an appearance."

Amanda looked at her watch. "It's still early. I'm sure I'm not needed here."

"Unless you want to catch up with Fred," Brendan said with mischief in his eyes.

"I think I've had all the news, thank you. Let's just mosey to the door and see if we can slip out without my parents noticing."

They wandered casually into the area of the sitting room closest to the front door and caught Simona's eye before explaining that they needed their coats and would wait in the vestibule. They slipped through the door and waited in the chilly space, sharing a kiss before the maid returned with their coats and a wink.

"We'd make a good espionage team," Amanda said as they walked to his car. "Believe me, my parents are vigilant."

"That's a good thing. Somehow, they always seem not to catch on to Louisa's antics."

"Who swiped my car to go see Rob."

Brendan laughed. "I hope things work out for them."

"What do you mean? That they get married? I don't know if that's the best ending for them."

"I don't know, either, but however it resolves, I hope not too many people are disappointed or hurt. They do come from two different worlds."

"As do we."

"But not in the same way. Different backgrounds, different religions, but we share the same values and that's what's important." He opened the passenger door for her.

"My concern is that maybe Louisa and Rob do share the same values. And they are ones that are sometimes questionable."

"I've never had much of a conversation with him, so I don't know what is important to him. Although judging by his attention to appearance, I guess he may have had a rough beginning in life and has had to make up for it with a successful business," Brendan said.

"At least now it's legitimate. So, I hope he makes scads of money because if he is still with Louisa, he'll need it."

Chapter 18

Amanda woke with a roaring headache, but not from the recital, which was sweet and comfortable being with Brendan's family. It was when she got back home and her parents' party was winding down, she noticed Cook, Mary and Simona were, too, after a long day and evening preparing, serving and then cleaning up. Since the remaining guests, including the Fosters, who liked to be the last to leave, had migrated to the sitting room, the dining room doors were closed and the clearing began.

There was a great deal of muttering from Cook, which was also part of the holiday party tradition since she would not hear of leaving until everything was washed up and put away. She did not consider the two maids capable of knowing how to properly stow the perishable food and kept a sharp eye on the washing up. Cook didn't dare criticize Amanda's paltry efforts at assisting and, to lighten the load in the punch bowl, the young woman decided to have a few glasses of what she thought might be apple juice. Suddenly, it was an even happier evening for her, and she fell into bed almost immediately, not bothering to wait up for Louisa. Her sister would have to fend for herself.

The next morning, they all had to fend for themselves since the staff had been given the day off after their double duty the day before. Amanda stumbled down to the kitchen in her robe and stupidly assumed that coffee would be waiting. No, but now she knew how to make it. Sort of. That process begun, she looked in the refrigerator and realized she hadn't eaten much the night before. Cold ham would be just fine. There were some puff pastry things that Cook had made and that would be a tolerable accompaniment. She sat at the butcher block table with her head in her hands waiting for the coffee to perk.

The clock in the kitchen informed her that she would be leaving for Hyannis again in an hour and she hadn't bathed or packed. She groaned. With any luck, the Warrens would be late arriving. They hadn't attended the party the night before, of course, as they were still in mourning, but she hoped they were as disorganized as she felt. Coffee poured, a plate of food assembled, she mounted the back stairs to her room to put warm clothes into a suitcase.

"Oh, drat!" Amanda had forgotten to bring the boxes of files from her father's office, except for the photos from the Scofield file, that she intended to look at more closely. She was wondering if Mrs. Warren knew who the woman posing next to the painting was. The rest of the files would have to wait for her return to Boston. This trip might involve some sorting of the Warrens' possessions but was mainly an emotional support effort on Amanda's part. They might be there two days at most and then back to Boston. What had begun as an attempt to take all of Mrs. Warren's things out of the house was now focused on removing August's belongings. As she had thought it best that he should not be present during the sorting, Mrs.

Warren hadn't informed him that they were going down to the Cape again.

"Don't you think you should let Uncle August know we'll be there?" Kitty asked her mother as they drove south.

"Absolutely not. I do not intend to be the recipient of another shouting episode from that man. Besides, I can never get in touch with him. He doesn't seem to answer his Boston telephone and I'm sure he's not at his Hyannis location, either."

"Where does he live in Hyannis?" Amanda asked from the back seat.

"He rents a room from a woman who used to be his nanny. You know how that relationship works."

Only having had a nursemaid when she was a baby, Amanda didn't know what she meant, but Mrs. Warren elucidated the situation.

"The boys were largely tended to by their nanny until their early teens because the elder Warrens were busy with their lives. Very old-fashioned British kind of thing. They spent more time with that woman than they did with their own parents. It seemed to suit everyone. Your father, being older, was the more favored child and he outgrew the nanny reliance early. August did not and in my opinion, that, and his natural tendencies, have led to a life of reliance on others and a lack of initiative. Why bother striving for goals when everything is handed to you?"

"So that's who she is," Kitty said. "I thought she was just a former servant. Well, I suppose she was, but now from what you've said, there is a much deeper tie."

Amanda thought it was odd that an adult man would continue to have such an attachment to a nanny, but she said nothing.

"Kitty, please turn up the heat," her mother asked.

"I don't know if a storm is coming in, but it's getting colder outside, and I've got the heat at full throttle. There's a blanket in the back seat, Amanda. Could you pass if forward and we'll get Mother covered up. I don't know why you dressed like that anyway."

"I've brought rough clothes for the work we're going to do, don't worry. But I'll have to meet with people at the bank, the attorney again, and who knows who else. I can't look like a bumpkin."

"I'm afraid those are the only type of clothes I brought," Amanda said with a laugh, hoping to lighten the mood and any tension between mother and daughter.

As they drove, the sky had the classic look of a snowstorm in the making so that by the time they were over the bridge flakes began to fall.

Mrs. Warren took a cigarette out of her purse and pushed in the car's lighter.

"Mother, you can't smoke in here. We'll suffocate with the windows up."

"I'll open the window a crack to let out the smoke."

"No, you can wait until we get there. It isn't much longer."

"I'm worried about the road being icy," Mrs. Warren said, putting the cigarette back in its case.

"It's fine. These are nice fluffy snowflakes. Not too wet."

But Amanda noticed that it was sticking, and all the lawns raked clean or covered with fallen leaves were now blanketed white. The bushes that landscaped the facades of the homes were white lumps and driveways, front paths, sidewalks and driveways were indistinguishable.

"It's coming down fast," Kitty said, turning the windshield wipers to their highest speed.

"Oh, look, we're coming to the turnoff. Only about five miles to go," her mother said.

As they headed south, they got behind an old truck going well below the speed limit, and it was only a two-lane road. They were forced to slow down.

"His tires are probably bald, and he'll be sliding all over road in no time."

"I thought you said the roads weren't slick."

Kitty looked in the rearview mirror at Amanda to ensure her complicity. "They're not. We'll be fine."

The truck slowed almost to a stop and then turned right off the road and Kitty accelerated, much to her mother's dismay. The older woman had one hand on the armrest and the other on the dashboard as Kitty tried to outrace the worsening storm. Twenty minutes later, with little visibility but also not much traffic, they pulled into the driveway of Belvedere.

"Thank goodness. That was a harrowing drive," Mrs. Warren said, hurrying out of the car and into the back door that led to the kitchen.

"We were sliding a bit, but I don't think she noticed," Kitty whispered to her friend.

"Thanks for the thrill ride," Amanda replied.

Rather than look for Josiah, if he were even in the house, the two young women unloaded the luggage themselves, their hats and shoulders covered with snow in the few minutes it took them to do so. They stomped their feet in the mud room, shook their heads and laughed at the mess of water they had flung on the floor.

Gertrude looked through the glass window of the kitchen door and shook her head. "Don't track that in, now. Take your boots off there," she said, going back to the stove.

"I'll bet she didn't say that to your mother," Amanda said.

"I wouldn't count on it," Kitty replied. "Let's see if we can get something hot to drink out of Gertrude. Oh, we should have stopped along the way to get whiskey—why didn't we think of it?"

"Do you even know who sells it down here?"

"I imagine just about everybody now. Wait, maybe there's some stashed away in my father's study."

They walked in their wool socks through the house to that room and Kitty riffled through the drawers of the desk and found nothing. They looked up as Mrs. Warren stood in the doorway.

"Looking for this?" she inquired, holding up a decanter. "Your father always had something in the study at home, if you recall. This was high up in a cabinet in the kitchen. I hope it's all right." She took the top off and sniffed. "Seems fine."

"I thought alcohol never went bad," Amanda said. "But what do I know?"

"I thought you might know a lot, with Louisa seeing a night-club owner," Kitty said.

Amanda didn't appreciate the comment but pretended that it didn't bother her. "It's a fully legitimate business these days and I believe he's going to make a fortune."

Mrs. Warren just raised her eyebrows. "How nice for him. Let's find some glasses."

She served them each a tot in a crystal tumbler, giving herself double, then sat in the larger armchair in the sitting room. It must have been her habitual seat as there was a cut glass cigarette case, silver lighter and ashtray on the table to the side. She lit up and, taking a deep drag, exhaled with a sigh of relief.

"How about if I have a cigarette, Mother?"

"No, you don't, Kitty. It's a terrible habit and I wish I hadn't started."

"Why did you?"

"It was considered the thing to do—what the modern young woman did. I'm sure I'll cut back again, but not just yet."

They sat sipping the whiskey and watching the smoke from her cigarette curl slowly to the ceiling.

"Peace at last," Mrs. Warren said.

It didn't last long. A few minutes later the doorbell rang.

"Kitty, would you get that?"

"Who in their right mind has come calling in a snowstorm?" she muttered as she did as she was told. She opened the vestibule door, then the front door proper and spoke briefly to someone before admitting him. He paused and pulled off galoshes, Kitty took his coat, and he entered the room. Mrs. Warren stood.

"Good afternoon, ma'am. I'm sorry to disturb you at this time, but I'm Nicholas Barber, you neighbor."

Mrs. Warren was puzzled. "What became of the Hiltons?"

"No, I'm your neighbor on the other side."

"Oh," she paused, registering who the man was. "May I offer you some whiskey?"

"No, thanks."

They stood for a moment before Mrs. Warren spoke. "You're the man with the trees on our property," she said sitting down. She did not offer him a seat, but he gestured in such a way as to indicate that he intended to sit and did so.

Amanda and Kitty exchanged looks.

"I wanted to say that I am sorry about the loss of your husband."

"Thank you," Mrs. Warren responded.

"I'm actually here on a business matter. I would like to buy your family's house."

"What?" Kitty said. Her mother was utterly still.

"What makes you think it's for sale?"

"Your brother-in-law has been talking about it for some time."

Mrs. Warren smiled. "Interesting." She took another puff of her cigarette. "However, it's not his house to sell."

He leapt out of the chair. "What?"

"This property belongs to me," she said evenly.

"What kind of game are you people playing here? First, your husband wants to take me to court and then your brother-in-law comes calling with a peace pipe."

"I don't know anything about that," she said.

"You think because you've been here forever and I'm an upstart that you can push me around and try to hoodwink me."

"I don't know anything about you, sir."

"Well, you'll know soon enough. You're going to pay me for those trees and the expenses associated with them as well as any legal fees when I win at court."

Mrs. Warren didn't respond. She stubbed out her cigarette.

Barber was very red in the face when he said, "I'll buy this property from you. At whatever price you want. You won't be able to maintain it much longer. I have a large family and am interested in acquiring several houses adjacent to mine for when the children get older for families of their own."

"Perhaps you could ask your neighbor on the other side."

"I can pay more than it's worth!" he shouted.

Mrs. Warren stood. "I'm afraid you don't know what it's worth to us. Good day." She had put her glass down and walked to the front entrance, opened it and stood waiting. Mr. Barber's face was red with embarrassment, but he managed to hold his head up as he went to the vestibule to put on his coat and galoshes. Amanda wondered if she were going to slam the door on him and then realized that the silence and waiting were much more effective.

"You haven't heard the last of this," he said, opening the front door and closing it behind him.

Mrs. Warren sat back down, and the young women could see her hands shaking. "Of all the nerve. First, he tries to encroach on our property, then he's scheming with August, who acted as if this house was so precious to him. All August was interested in was the money. As usual." She took another cigarette out of the case and lit it. "I was prepared to have August come in and remove his things but right now I feel like throwing his ridiculous tennis trophies and other bits of his juvenile success, the apex of his life, I may add, out the window into a snow drift."

"Brava!" Kitty said, applauding.

The comment managed to get a smile out of her mother.

"Would you get me a glass of water, dear?" she asked.

"I'll get it," Amanda offered, wanting them to revel in their small victory alone. Gertrude wasn't in the kitchen, so Amanda opened cabinets looking for a glass. Glancing toward the back stairs, she saw a muddy puddle on the floor. Surely, she and Kitty hadn't tracked that in when they arrived because they had removed their boots in the mud room.

"Can I help you, Miss?" Gertrude asked, from the door to the dining room. She followed Amanda's line of sight to the puddle. "What on earth?" she said and took a cloth that hung from the oven door handle and wiped it up. "It's all I can do to keep this place clean with everyone coming and going."

"I was just looking for a glass for Mrs. Warren. Here, I think I've found one." As she took it from the cabinet, she could feel the eyes of the woman on her. A sudden thought came to her that someone had come in the back door recently and it wasn't and of them. Had Gertrude let August into the house? Had he overheard the conversation in the sitting room? Or was it someone else? But she said nothing and decided to tell her suspicions to Kitty out of earshot of the housekeeper.

Chapter 19

Amanda waited until she and Kitty had carried the luggage upstairs to share her concerns.

"It's probably none of my business, but I think something nefarious is going on."

"I'll say," Kitty replied, snapping open her suitcase.

"No, listen. There was a puddle of water by the back stairs in the kitchen just now."

"I don't understand."

"Someone with wet shoes or boots came in through the back door while we were in the sitting room and went up the back stairs."

"Are you sure it wasn't what we tracked in?"

"Of course not. Gertrude had us take our boots off in the mud room. Could it have been Josiah?"

"No. He doesn't go upstairs unless there is something heavy to be moved. And certainly not with wet boots. Do you think my uncle came in? We didn't lock the door behind us. Was Gertrude in the kitchen?"

"I don't know where she was. She just kind of appeared behind me and made a fuss when she saw what I saw."

Kitty bit her lip. "This is going to sound ridiculous, but maybe we should search up here to see if he or someone else got into the house." She went to her closet, rummaged around and took out a tennis racket.

"What are you doing?" Amanda asked.

"Well, I don't have a gun, and this could pass for a weapon."

"I don't suppose you have another in there," Amanda said.

"No. You'll have to whack him with a sturdy wooden hanger."

"I don't know whether to laugh or be scared."

"Come on, we'll start at the end of the hall. My parents' room. If he's up to no good, he'll be prowling around in there. Stealing jewelry if he hasn't rifled through everything already."

They walked softly down the carpeted hall and out of habit, Kitty knocked on the closed door and then shut her eyes at her clumsy mistake.

"Oh, well," she said, and they went into the dark room. She walked to the nearest window and pulled the drape aside slightly. "Would you look at that storm?"

Amanda followed and was surprised at how much snow had fallen since their short time in the house. "Who's that?" she whispered, pointing to someone trudging across the front yard.

"I can hardly see. I don't know who it is." They watched the figure disappear around the side of the house. "Come on. I'll look under the beds, and you look in the closet."

"No!" Amanda said quietly yet forcefully. "We'll do this together."

They bent down and lifted the bed skirts up and saw nothing but a pair of slippers. They approached the closet in the corner and Amanda felt her stomach clutch. Kitty walked slowly, took the knob in her hand with the tennis racket raised in her other hand and whipped the door open, yelling, "Ha!"

Amanda let out a scream at the noise, but seeing nothing, she hit her friend on the arm.

"Sorry. Element of surprise," Kitty said.

"Are you going to do that when you open every closed door?" Amanda asked, getting no response.

Kitty walked to the bathroom whose door was open and she looked around and shrugged her shoulders.

"How many more rooms to go?"

"Uncle August's old room—or shrine, as we call it. You'll see what I mean. My room, your room and two other guest rooms."

"This is agonizing," Amanda said. "But if the person went up the back stairs, maybe they're in one of the maids' rooms. I mean, I don't see any wet footprints here."

"I see your observant and deductive mind at work."

Amanda didn't know if her friend was being sarcastic or not but followed her as they made the rounds through the other rooms on the second floor, looking behind doors, drapes, under beds, in closets and bathrooms as they went. They even looked in the walk-in linen closet which afforded enough space for someone to hide.

"And now, we enter the shrine," Kitty said in mock tones.

It resembled the other bedrooms except the drapes were closed and the shades down. Once Kitty had opened them, it was a bright space that looked as if it belonged to someone a great deal younger than her uncle.

"The trophies," Kitty said, gesturing to more than a dozen figures mounted on wooden bases and two engraved silver cups. "Tennis. August only stopped playing a few years ago after he tore his something-or-other in his knee. The college pennant," she said motioning with her other hand. "No model airplanes, I'm afraid. I guess we'd better check the closet—gosh, I hope Uncle August isn't hiding in there."

"Stop it," Amanda said, feeling jittery enough.

But there was no one hiding in the closet or in the adjoining bathroom.

"Up we go," Kitty said. "We'd better take the back stairs. Now, come to think of it, once the person—if there was a person—came up the stairs this far, his or her boots would no longer be wet. Or perhaps they took them off. Or perhaps nobody came upstairs but just stood for a bit in the kitchen chatting to Gertrude."

"That makes me feel ridiculous."

"Sorry, no offense intended."

They had reached the third floor, which had a long corridor with two doors on either side. Opening the first, Kitty turned on the light to show two single beds covered with bedsheets to protect them from dust and one small closet whose door was ajar. There were no bed skirts to pull aside and by just leaning over, they could see nothing underneath except a few dust balls.

The next room revealed the same arrangement of furniture and silence, likewise the third. The fourth was locked and Amanda looked at Kitty in alarm, pointing to the door.

"That's Gertrude's room when she stays here."

"And she keeps it locked?" Amanda asked.

Kitty shrugged.

A large bathroom intended to serve all the residents of that floor revealed no hidden perpetrators, and they came back out into the corridor.

"What's that door go to?" Amanda asked.

"That's the attic. Haven't been up there in ages." She put her hand on the doorknob. "It's locked. Good luck to anyone who would want to hide in there. No heat whatsoever. But we'll have to brave it to look through things and see if anything should be returned to Uncle August or tossed out. My recollection is there was a bit of broken furniture."

"So, we've exhausted all possible hiding places?" Amanda asked.

"There's the cellar," Kitty said.

"We should have thought of the basement right off the bat. We'd better be thorough and do a full reconnaissance."

"I should make sure that Josiah really did get the locks changed, that Gertrude keeps the doors locked at all times and doesn't let Uncle August in under any circumstances."

They trooped down the back stairs to the kitchen where there was a separate door to the basement. Amanda considered that the wet footprints could have gone downstairs as easily as up.

Gertrude gave a puzzled glance at the tennis racket but turned back to her work at the stove.

Although they had turned on the light, when they descended the stairs, the bare bulb in the middle of the first room cast little illumination and the corners were in deep shadow.

"Why are cellars always so gloomy and creepy?" Kitty asked.

"We should have brought a flashlight. I could go back up and get one."

"And leave me here alone? Absolutely not. Gosh, it's cold."

There were the clerestory windows to the outside but with the snow piling up, visibility was limited. Pieces of furniture covered in dust littered the room as well as some metal objects on the floor, but seeing no disturbance in the dust, they surmised that no one had come this way.

"Let's go," Kitty said.

There was a bang from beyond the closed door ahead of them.

"What's through there?" Amanda asked.

"The furnace room and the coal chute, which is dark and scary."

"I'm just going to take a peek," Amanda said and opening the door was hit by a blast of cold air as well as the heat from the furnace. "Look," she said pointing to steps that led upward to the cellar's access from the outside. One of the flap doors had been left open and there was snow on the steps and footprints in the snow, both coming and going.

"That's supposed to be latched from the outside," Kitty said. "I wonder if Josiah came in this way and forgot to fasten it when he was done."

"Unless someone else came in."

"But why? Do you think they heard us in the other room and fled just now?"

"I'm going to take a look," Amanda said and went up the steps, pushed the banging door further open and stepped outside. Footsteps led away from the house although no one was in sight; not that much could be seen in the storm. She went back down the stairs.

"Do you think we should tell your mother?"

"Absolutely not. She's got enough on her mind. Let me make sure the house is secure and we can lock the cellar door from inside the kitchen. If someone breaks in from the outside doors at least they won't be able to come upstairs."

Chapter 20

The storm raged on, and the two young women were on edge from their recent discovery.

"Let's make ourselves useful—or busy, at least," Amanda suggested, not feeling comfortable thinking about intruders.

"I'll see if my mother feels up to sorting through some things in the attic." But after a short conversation, she determined that her mother had been unsettled by the neighbor's brash offer of buying the house and all she wanted to do was go to her room and lie down.

"I'll find the key," Kitty said and after some searching in unlikely places, came back with a skeleton key that she held up triumphantly.

"We probably could have picked that lock if we knew that's what it took," Amanda said.

"You know how to pick a lock?" Kitty asked.

"A little," she responded evasively. She had come across something in the library a few months earlier written by an ex-thief explaining how the process worked, and she not only devoured the material, but also took to practicing on the various doors in her home. She found that the common notion that you could open a locked door with a bobby pin was ridiculous and in reading further, she learned that special tools were required. She was dying to find a set but didn't dare ask Brendan where to get one or he would become suspicious of her intentions.

"I don't want to know how you know that. This is much easier." She turned the key, and they climbed the steep wooden stairs, turning on a light switch as they went.

"I hope your mother doesn't mind that I'm poking around in your family's things."

"Most of this if from my grandmother, who thought that things that were out of fashion would someday come back into vogue. Just look at that poor divan." Kitty stepped forward and lifted a dusty sheet from a heavy piece of furniture with dark wood and darker upholstery. "Ugh. Although it's hideous, it was made by some fine craftsmen, and it was probably that which she appreciated."

"I suppose you could have it recovered," Amanda suggested.

Kitty looked at her with disdain. "I have no idea how they managed to get it up here or how anyone could get it back down. It probably looks even more dreadful in daylight. So here it shall remain." She replaced the sheet with a flick of her wrist and coughed at the dust she had stirred up.

"What do you think is up here that is worth sorting through?"

"Once upon a time, there was an agreement that each member of the family had a certain spot where they could store things. Here's mine." She led them to the back of the room by the small window. "Oh, look, my doll carriage."

"I know you're not here to clean out the attic, but really, Kitty, why are you holding on to that?"

"Sentimental. And because Mother is sure that someday I will be married and have children and my little girl will fall in love with the doll carriage, too. Although she will probably look at the wrecked thing and wonder why someone couldn't have bought her a new, shiny one."

"You seem to know what your nonexistent daughter will be like already."

"Here are some old school books which I really ought to get rid of, but let's look at Uncle August's stash. Those are the things that ought to leave the house. And Uncle August with them."

She moved back to a wardrobe and opened the doors. "His school uniform. What was he thinking? Everyone hates their old school uniform and here he has saved his. And some moth-eaten letter sweater from some sport or other." She pushed the hangers along the rod and said, "A raccoon coat! Now this would be worth taking," she said, pulling it out but holding it away from her body. "As long as it doesn't have critters in it. And a ukulele! Uncle August must have been the cat's pajamas."

"The bees' knees," Amanda said, and they laughed at how absurd fashions used to be.

Kitty pulled a framed group photograph from the back of the wardrobe. "He was a handsome devil, I'll grant you that." She used a handkerchief to wipe the dust off the glass. "We'll let him sort through all this and take what he wants. But I want to show you some of my grandmother's clothes."

She closed the wardrobe and went to the other side of the attic to a larger wardrobe decorated with painted roses. "This came from their old house where they didn't have closets." She opened the doors. "Look at this." She pulled a cloth away from a beaded gown with a high neck. "Isn't that glorious? Feel how heavy it is, though."

Amanda lifted the skirt with one hand. "And they probably wore corsets, too. Thank goodness we are spared those tortures."

"And this was her wedding dress. Isn't it lovely?" Kitty said, unpinning a different fabric clothing bag. "I think these must be real pearls," she said, looking at them closely.

"You should wear that for your wedding," Amanda suggested.

"First, I'll need a groom. And it's way too fussy for me and everyone would know it was an old thing. I bet it would fall apart if you tried to dry clean it."

"Here are some of her evening clothes," Kitty said, unzipping a wide bag that had several long dresses inside. "She loved color and pattern."

Amanda's eye was caught by the distinctive paisley. "I've seen that dress before," she said.

"How is that even possible?"

"I know, but I remember where I saw it. It was in a photo taken of your grandmother seated in front of the painting that's at Scofield's Gallery."

"Really? Where did you see it?"

"It was among the files that the investigator had assembled for Scofield as a means of verifying the family's ownership. I brought it with me. The pattern of the dress is unmistakable."

"I think we could use the word 'gaudy,' even if it was the fashion then."

Kitty carefully zipped up the bag and made sure the other garments were properly covered before closing the wardrobe, whose latch didn't seem to catch. She tried again and it still didn't close. She gave one last push and the lock caught and there was a thud from behind the piece of furniture as something fell to the ground.

"Oops." Kitty made a face. "I hope I didn't knock the back out of this old thing. The moths will get in." She put her hand around the side and looked puzzled before shifting something into the light.

"Oh, look! How clever. Someone made a copy of our painting."

"It's a replica of the Turner that's in Scofield's gallery," Amanda said. She looked at it again.

"I didn't know this existed. Do you think Turner painted two exactly the same?"

"I doubt it. I've read that some artists churn out multiple copies of their work—the more modern, commercial folks. But this man painted in the last century, and I don't know if it was common then."

"Since Scofield has the original, we could hang this one up where the real one used to be. I do miss looking at the sails in the mist and fog." Shifting it, she said, "It's awfully heavy."

Between the two of them, they were able to extricate it and move it to a position under the light.

"Whatever it is, it's lovely. And so like the original," Amanda said. "I'm not speaking from memory; I was at Scofield's and saw the original on display."

"Let's take it downstairs. Mother will be pleased to have some semblance of how things used to be."

They alternately lifted and dragged it over to the stairs and carefully carried it down the attic stairs and slowly down the other two flights to the study where the original had been hung.

"It's a bit too heavy for us to lift and hang it. Let's put it against the wall and deal with it tomorrow." Kitty looked out the window. "Loo, it's stopped snowing!"

They surveyed the yard populated with white lumps that were bushes underneath and the path from the house to the driveway which Josiah was busy shoveling.

"And we can get out!" Kitty said.

"Why? Where did you want to go?"

"The Christmas tree lighting ceremony on the village green, of course. I think it starts about five-thirty. The school choir will sing carols and there will be hot chocolate."

"How do you know?"

"They do it every year although we're seldom down here to see it."

"NO HOT BUTTERED RUM?" Amanda asked.

"Sorry. But we can take the car unless you'd rather walk into town. It's only a few blocks, as you saw when we came in, but my guess is that the snow will not have been plowed or shoveled."

"Car it is. Do you think your mother would like to go?"

"She might but I don't think she wants to face other people just yet."

When Kitty told her mother her intentions, she was met with opposition.

"You don't know what people are saying about us," Mrs. Warren said.

"What do you mean?"

"I think August has wound people up about us inheriting the house and who knows what malicious rumors he may be spreading."

Kitty was aghast. "Do you know anything for sure or are you just assuming?"

"The sheriff wanted to come by again tonight, if that's any indication."

"Don't you think he wants to conclude things?"

"I got the impression that the investigation was ongoing."

Kitty just stared at her mother. "Well, I'm going to hold my head up high. Come on, Amanda."

Amanda did not like being put between her friend and Mrs. Warren, but she capitulated and agreed to go to the event. It was fully dark by the time they left, and Kitty drove at a snail's pace although she maintained that the streets were not icy, just snowy. From a distance they could see people with flashlights gathering at the village green since all the streetlights had been turned off in anticipation of the big moment. Behind the moving beams stood a tall evergreen tree and excited children or parents occasionally turned their lights in that direction, which reflected off shiny ornaments.

"How in the world did they decorate that tree?" Amanda asked as they trudged from the parked car to the assembled, buzzing group.

"The volunteer firefighters do it every year. They may be the only people with ladders long enough."

They joined the group of parents and neighbors a short way from the children who stood in front of the tree. The talking became whispers and then there was silence. A voice from in front of the choir called for attention.

"Ladies and Gentlemen, Hyannis officially announces the arrival of Christmas."

Suddenly, the tree exploded with light, and the crowd gasped and applauded. The children were supposed to be facing forward to follow the choir director, but most of them were still gaping at the vision behind them. He blew on his pitch pipe, which got their attention, and holding up his hands he looked expectantly, lowered his hands and they began to sing 'Away in a Manger.'

Kitty and Amanda smiled at each other as they observed most of the children singing while others were too absorbed with looking over their shoulders at the giant tree. They sang about four more songs with the families and bystanders joining in before ending with 'Jingle Bells.' A boy in the front held up harness bells and when they shouted, 'Hey' at the end, he shook the bells vigorously to applause.

"Ladies and gentlemen. Choir and Director, please have some hot chocolate and cookies."

Whoever was doing the announcing did not have to repeat himself and there was almost a stampede of young people over to the tables set up for refreshments. The adults waited their turn, parents catching up to their children and breaking off in small groups. A few people noticed Kitty in the crowd and gave her wide berth while others whispered behind their hands. One woman came up and stood in front of her.

"I wanted to say how sorry I am about your father. And pay no heed to what the gossips are saying." She nodded her head, having done her good deed for the day. Kitty turned and pulled Amanda with her.

"Let's go home."

To her credit, Kitty did not cry over the incident but instead was furious as they made their way back to the car.

"How dare she say that?"

"Who was that?" Amanda asked.

"Someone who runs one of the stores on Main Street. She probably hears all the tittle tattle that goes around town. And in her special way, she wanted to point out that we're the topic of gossip but that she's not responsible for spreading it."

They got in the car and slammed the doors shut.

"Not a word to my mother."

"Of course not! Mum's the word."

They drove the short distance back at a greater speed than they had come, and neither felt any need to talk about it further. The car parked, they went into the mud room and stomped the snow off their boots, removed them and walked in stocking feet into the kitchen. Gertrude was at the stove and, knowing who it was, didn't bother turning to see them come in.

"Dinner in a half hour unless you've stuffed yourselves with cookies and hot cocoa."

Kitty didn't respond and stormed out of the room, passing her mother on the stairs. Mrs. Warren looked at Amanda and was about to ask what the matter was.

"I think she got her socks wet. We'll be down as soon as we change."

"Then you'll tell me all about your day."

Dinner was a miserable affair, with Amanda desperately trying to think of some topic of conversation. She had no intention of relating the remark made at the tree lighting ceremony nor the looks that people had given Kitty. The discovery of the painting was Kitty's story to tell. And there was no way she would share their escapade of looking for the phantom intruder whose only existence was a puddle of water in the kitchen and a flapping cellar door to the outside.

"I'm reading quite an interesting book," Amanda began and then took a bite of chicken, hoping to buy time to think of something. Kitty had been pushing her food around on her plate with a sullen expression. Now all eyes were on Amanda, and she coughed as if choking and held up her hand to take a sip of water. She glared at Kitty, willing her to join the conversation.

"The children were charmingly out of tune, as usual. The tree was well decorated, and it seemed the entire town was there."

"That's nice. Did you see anyone we know?"

"Not really. As you can imagine, it was dark in anticipation of the big reveal of the lights on the tree coming to life."

They were almost finished when the doorbell rang. Gertrude came through the dining room to the sitting room and the front door, looking peeved at having her dinner in the kitchen interrupted.

"The sheriff is here," she said to Mrs. Warren before disappearing back into the kitchen.

Mrs. Warren sighed at the disruption even though she knew he would be coming and walked slowly to the sitting room, Kitty and Amanda following. The man was surprised to see all three women and looked uncomfortable.

"Perhaps I should talk to you alone," he suggested.

"I think they can stay," Mrs. Warren said almost daring him.

Everyone sat.

"I just had a few questions to ask you to follow up, you know."

Mrs. Warren waited.

"When did your husband leave your home on the day he came down here?"

"About eight o'clock in the morning. I knew he was coming down here. He was certainly dressed as if he were."

"Did you pack him a lunch or something to eat for the trip?"

"What an odd question. I am not in the habit of packing my husband a lunch."

"Was there anything in the car that he might have eaten?"

"How could I possibly know that? Why are you asking me these questions?"

"You know your husband was poisoned. And there are only a few people who could have administered it to him."

"Are you accusing me of poisoning my husband? Don't be ridiculous. I last saw him at breakfast when he ate what I ate. If he was on the road he may have stopped or perhaps he had something here. He may have dined with someone for all I know." She was furious and did not hold back. "I think it's time for you to leave."

The sheriff sheepishly stood up, nodded and crept out the front door.

Chapter 21

During the night, the wind picked up, rattling the shutters and waking Amanda several times. She heard tapping and, leaning over to look out the window, saw the thin, gnarled limb of one of the elms hitting the glass. There was a moment when she considered opening the window and breaking off the branch but thought better of it and went back to bed, partially covering her head with a pillow.

The household was awakened early the next morning by loud screams that came from the first floor. Shortly thereafter, Mrs. Warren, Kitty and Amanda ran down the stairs in their night-clothes, following the source of the noise to the kitchen. Gertrude was standing at the open back door with her hands on either side of her face. Mrs. Warren whirled her around.

"Stop it! Stop it!"

When she didn't stop screaming, Mrs. Warren shook her by the shoulders. She collapsed on the floor and began to sob.

"Who is it? Josiah?" Amanda asked, peering around Mrs. Warren, who had grabbed the open door.

"It's Uncle August," Kitty said. "He's actually frozen."

They took in the scene for a moment before Amanda assisted Gertrude up from the floor, through the mud room and into a kitchen chair. She got a glass of water and gave it to the woman before returning to mother and daughter who seemed unable to move.

"Let me make sure," Amanda offered, putting her fingers alongside his neck which had been covered by a dusting of snow. No pulse, and his skin was as cold as the air outside. "Let's call the sheriff."

She had to usher Mrs. Warren and Kitty back into the house before she could close the door.

"I'll do it," Kitty volunteered.

Mrs. Warren sat down shivering, either from the cold or the sight of her inert brother-in-law. "I had Josiah change the locks. Do you think he was trying to come in and had a seizure or something and froze to death?"

"Why don't we get dressed," Amanda suggested, helping Mrs. Warren up the stairs. "We don't know what happened yet."

As she put on warm clothes, Amanda wondered if any of the noises she heard in the night had been August trying to get into the house. Was it only the branch that had tapped at her window or had he been outside the kitchen door, trying to get someone's attention but too weak to call out or hammer on the door. She went to Kitty's room and found the door open and the bedroom empty. However, she could hear Kitty whispering to her mother, perhaps helping her dress. Or was some secret being shared?

The sheriff arrived soon and by that time Gertrude had regained some function, made coffee and put cups and saucers out on the kitchen worktable before sinking back into a chair.

Amanda went to the door to the yard and greeted the sheriff and told him what they knew so far.

"And who are you exactly?" he asked, peeved that no one had told him previously.

"I'm a friend of the family. Of Kitty, actually."

He muttered something and then said, "I'd better get the doctor. May I use the telephone?"

"Certainly," Amanda said, leading him into the kitchen where one of the extensions was located. He knew the number by heart, dialed it and had a brief conversation before hanging up.

"Would you like some coffee?" Amanda asked.

He nodded and blew out a breath of exasperation before sitting down across from Gertrude.

"How are you holding up?"

She just stared at him as if that were the stupidest question she had ever heard.

"Where's your boy?"

"Upstairs. Sleeping."

Amanda looked from one to the other. "Boy?"

"Her son, Daniel."

"Here? In this house?" Kitty asked.

"Where else was he supposed to go?" Gertrude asked.

Amanda looked at Kitty, who didn't seem surprised by the information. "Your mystery intruder. The puddle on the floor?" she elaborated.

"Aha."

"Well, I for one am hungry. I'll make some breakfast," Kitty said. She didn't show concern about her uncle's demise as she went to the refrigerator and took out a bowl of eggs, butter and a bottle of milk.

"You know how to cook?" Amanda asked.

"It's just scrambled eggs. Of course, I know how to make them. There are times I would have gone hungry from awful food. A hot plate and some eggs go a long way."

"Let me watch," Amanda said, eager to learn.

"Why don't you cut some bread and we can have toast?"

In a short time, the buttered bread was in the hottest part of the oven while the eggs were being stirred on the stove top. Mrs. Warren heard the noise in the kitchen and came back in, only to leave and set the table for five people.

"Best to bring the plates in here. And better make it for six," Kitty said over her shoulder.

They moved from the kitchen into the dining room to eat the hastily prepared meal. A sound at the door from the hallway announced the mystery guest, Daniel, who politely said hello and sat next to his mother. With the shock of the day, the appearance of the young man didn't seem to startle anyone, least of all Amanda, who then recognized him as the figure she had seen crossing the yard in the snow. They ate quickly in silence until there was a knock at the back door and the sheriff got up.

"It'll be the doctor." He left the room.

They continued eating and Kitty went back to the kitchen to retrieve the coffee.

Amanda couldn't get out of her mind the image of August at the back door, tapping, scraping his hands on the wood to get someone's attention until he fell back, died and then became frozen. Or was he injured and incapacitated and then froze to death? Either one was a horrible way to die.

The meal finished, Gertrude had come to herself and was able to get up and clear the table with the assistance of her son. When they left the room, Amanda asked Kitty, "Has he been in the house all this time, do you think?"

"Who knows. Gertrude has her own place, of course, but since she had to be here while we were in town, she probably temporarily closed her house up. Turned off the heat and all that."

Amanda didn't know what was expected of them at that point. She imagined that they were supposed to wait there until the sheriff came back in, which he did a few minutes later with the doctor. The doctor tipped his hat to Mrs. Warren.

"Terrible accident," she said.

"I don't think so," the sheriff responded. "He was hit on the back of the head with a heavy object. I imagine that killed him instantly. Someone then rolled him over onto his back. Why, I don't know. Perhaps to disguise the fact that it was a violent attack." They both left the room.

"How horrible," Mrs. Warren said.

The sheriff returned holding something that looked like weathered wood in both hands. "Do you recognize this?"

"Yes," Mrs. Warren said, turning white.

"I believe this is the murder weapon," the sheriff said.

"It's one of my sculptures. Somebody stole it!"

"And hit your brother-in-law on the skull and killed him. I think we need to have a little talk, don't you?" he said to Mrs. Warren.

"I'll call the ambulance," the doctor said, returning to the kitchen.

"Where can we have a conversation?" the sheriff asked, no longer cowed by Mrs. Warren.

She suggested the study and while going through the sitting room, picked up her cigarettes. The radiators had been turned off in some of the lesser used rooms, including the study, and she went behind the desk to turn the knob and gasped.

"What is it?" the sheriff asked.

"It's the family's painting. What's it doing here?"

The sheriff wasn't interested in the family's artwork or her confusion at seeing it and asked her to sit down so he could ask her some questions.

"Where were you last night?"

"Here, of course. We had dinner and I went to bed early." She lit a cigarette and inhaled deeply,

"You didn't hear someone at the back door?"

"My room is at the other side of the house—how could I?"

"Did your brother-in-law have free access to the house?"

"He used to, but I had the locks changed."

"Why is that?"

"Because I inherited the house. He was angry about that and came bursting in to vent his anger at me. I didn't feel safe that he was able to come and go as he pleased."

"Safe? Why not?"

"He could be an erratic person. He was furious about the change in my husband's will and he's a big man. Was."

"Did you feel you needed to subdue him by hitting him over the head with your artwork?"

"No, of course not. I can hardly lift the thing."

"You made it," he pursued. So, someone else helped you?"

"No! I didn't move it and I didn't kill August. I don't know why he was at the house sometime during the night and I don't know who wanted to kill him."

"I think there were plenty of people who wanted to kill him. But probably only one succeeded. That's all for now. But I'd like to talk to the other residents and guests in your house. Let's start with your daughter."

"She had nothing to do with this."

"How do you know? Do you share a bedroom? Was the other girl sleeping in the same room with her?" He gave an awful smirk.

Mrs. Warren got up abruptly. "I'll go get her," and she quickly left the room.

Kitty appeared a few minutes later, her eyes wide with curiosity but not intimidated by the man. "You wanted to talk to me?" she inquired.

"Please. Sit down. First, do you sleep alone?"

"Yes," she said, puzzled by his question.

"Not in the same room as your mother or your friend?"

"That's right."

"Did you hear anything unusual during the night?"

"It was windy, and I heard the usual creaking and banging when that happens."

"Did you hear anyone knocking at the back door or calling out?"

"Certainly not. If I had, I would have responded to it."

"Did you get up at any point in the night, to get a drink of water or use the bathroom, for example?"

"No. I usually sleep soundly. Except for the wind last night."

"What was your relationship with your uncle?"

"The normal uncle and niece relationship. We didn't see him often although he lived in Boston most of the time."

"But he had a place down here, too, didn't he?"

"Yes, he rents from someone. Haven't you been to that place?"

"Not yet."

"Not even after knowing that my father was poisoned? I should think he might be your primary suspect," Kitty said.

"And why is that?"

She blew out a gust of frustration. "Because my father owned the house and my uncle assumed he would inherit it. Perhaps finding out that my father created a new will that excluded him made him angry and he acted on that information."

"Do you know if your uncle knew the will had been changed?"

"I don't. My mother and I certainly didn't know it. My father did it through Mr. Baldwin down here in Hyannis rather than in Boston, so we had no idea."

"Hmm," was the most the sheriff could say. "I may need to talk to you again."

"Fine. But you won't get any different information from me than what I have already supplied." She left with her head held high.

"Just a minute," the sheriff said. "Have your friend come in next."

Kitty muttered under her breath at having to be the messenger for the man she considered incompetent, but she let Amanda know it was her turn.

"And who are you, exactly?" the sheriff began.

"Amanda Burnside. I'm Kitty's friend. I agreed to come down here and help them sort out some of the family's belongings."

"Why, if there had been no change in ownership?"

"They didn't know that on our first visit here. So, this trip really wasn't necessary except that Mrs. Warren wanted to make sure that her brother-in-law took possession of his things. And she wanted to talk to Mr. Baldwin, the attorney."

"She threw August out?"

"I don't know if that's the proper description. The family has lived here for a long time, so figuring out who owns what might have taken some time. And he didn't live here, from what I know."

"Why did she want to talk to the attorney?

"You'll have to ask her that," Amanda answered, becoming peeved at his attitude.

"What did you hear last night?"

"The wind, branches scraping along the windows, other creaks and noises of an old house," she said.

"Nobody knocking, calling, rapping at the door."

"I wouldn't characterize what I heard as that. It seemed like normal sounds outside on a windy night. If he had been at the front door or the back door, I wouldn't have been able to hear him as the room I'm staying in is not near either of the entrances."

The sheriff rubbed his chin that hadn't been shaved yet and it made an unpleasant rasping sound. "I might need to talk to you again."

Amanda got up, but he took hold of her arm as she was about to pass by.

"Did any of you touch the body?"

She pulled her arm away. "I put my fingers on his neck to feel for a pulse, that's all. And obviously, there wasn't one." She rubbed her arm where his hand had laid and left the room. "What an odious man," she muttered when she was well out of his hearing.

Gertrude was called in next and given the same sort of questions about hearing noises in the night.

"I'm staying in a room on the third floor. You can't hear anything up there except the squirrels in the attic."

The sheriff gave her a look as if wondering if she were pulling his leg.

"I'm serious. When the weather gets cold, they're not interested in nesting in the hollow of a tree when they can find a way in through the roof to the much warmer attic. I heard them scratching around. You know you can't poison them, or they'll die in the walls and that will be a proper stink. You just have to wait until the weather warms up a bit and they go to get a nest ready for when the young ones are born."

"Quite an expert on squirrels, are you?"

Gertrude ignored his taunt.

"You're the one who found him, is that right?"

"Yes."

"What time was that?"

"After I came down to get things ready for breakfast."

"He was on the ground outside so how did you know to open the door and find him?"

"You can't see to the outside well from the kitchen, only from the mud room. I went in there because I usually do, first thing. To make sure everything is as it should be. I went to the door to look out and see how deep the snow was and if Josiah would need to be called to shovel more."

"Couldn't you see how deep the snow was from your upstairs window?"

Gertrude was holding her ground. "You can't tell by looking down at it from up there. You should know better."

"What's your son doing here?"

"Where is he to go? You and Mr. Warren put him away and once he got out when summer was over, there were either no jobs or nobody wanted to hire him."

"Plenty of fishing boats still going out."

"We're not fisherfolk."

"Why isn't he at your place?"

"It's warmer here and I don't have to pay for the heat. Besides, after Mr. Warren died, there was no way I would stay here on my own."

The sheriff scowled. "Send in your boy."

Gertrude glowered at him. "He's got a name, you know."

It was a few minutes before Daniel came into the study, already on the defensive.

"Have a seat, Junior," the sheriff gestured at one of the chairs.

"The name's Daniel."

"I know what your name is. So, you made it out, did you? It was supposed to teach you a lesson, but you seem as surly as you ever were."

Daniel didn't reply.

"You've had free run of the place with the family gone, isn't that so?"

No answer.

"You can get in and out of the garage where we found some arsenic. Is that what you used on Rupert Warren?"

"No, I didn't have a beef with him. I found out it was his brother who ratted me out."

"Ha!" The sheriff pointed his finger at Daniel. "So, you had a motive to kill August Warren!"

"I could have, but I didn't. How would I know he was even here? He told my mother he was going back to Boston."

"Great pals, are they? Even though he did you wrong."

"Not anymore," Daniel said, then quickly shut his mouth when he realized he had said too much.

"Your mother lets him in the house on some pretext and you bash in his head with one of those monstrosities that Mrs. Warren made."

"That's not what happened," Daniel said, standing up.

"That's how it looks to me. I'm taking you in to the station. And don't try to run away," the sheriff said, seeing the look in the boy's eyes. "Don't worry, it'll be warm there, too."

Chapter 22

The sheriff marched Daniel out through the dining room and Gertrude put her hand over her mouth and closed her eyes. Everyone else stood up puzzled at events.

"You can't," Amanda said. "Mr. Warren had other enemies. There's the neighbor next door who wanted to buy this property because August implied that the house would soon be his, but, of course, that wasn't the case."

Kitty spoke up. "My uncle had money worries. Maybe he borrowed money from someone who was angry that he wouldn't be paid back."

"All very well and good. But this young man is coming in for additional questioning. He's been on the lam long enough."

"I'm not on the lam. I served my time and you're not going to frame me for something I didn't do." He pushed the sheriff, who fell onto Gertrude, who screamed and hit the man.

"Get off of me, you horrible man," she yelled.

"You can't assault an officer of the law!" he shot back.

"You're the one who assaulted me."

By the time they got their arms, legs and insults untangled, Daniel had dashed through the kitchen door, locking it behind him, then out the mud room door and past the newly arri ed ambulance men who just stared at the retreating figure.

There was fumbling of the doorknob before Gertrude ever so slowly produced the key. The furious sheriff was going to give chase on foot before deciding to follow the young man in his car. But it was blocked by the ambulance attendants who had been trying to maneuver the frozen body onto a stretcher.

"Forget about him for now. Move your dang vehicle!"

The attendants looked at the doctor, whose mouth was open at the scene taking place, not understanding what was required of him.

"Move it!"

One attendant dropped his end of the stretcher and scrunched through the deep snow as quickly as he could but turned around. "You've got the keys," he said to the other. The other man dug in his pocket and lobbed them to his partner who fumbled and dropped them in the snow.

The sheriff flapped his hands against his side in frustration, yelling obscenities at the two men as they dug in the snow for the keys.

"Oh, forget it!" the sheriff yelled. "I'll be back!" he said to no one in particular.

"If it weren't so awful, it would almost be funny," Amanda said.

"Nothing funny about that man," Gertrude said. "Or about any of this."

It seemed a good moment for them to leave the housekeeper to her thoughts in the kitchen while they retreated to other parts of the house.

"Mrs. Warren, would you mind if I made a long-distance call?" Amanda asked.

"Of course not. Who knows how much longer we'll have to stay here. But Kitty, please explain what the painting is doing in the study." Mother and daughter went into the study where Amanda could hear them talking. She went to the upstairs hall where there was a telephone extension and called the operator and gave her the number in Boston.

"Well, I was wondering if you would ever call," Brendan said when he answered.

"I can't talk long and certainly not in much more than a whisper."

"I don't like the sound of that."

"August Warren was found dead outside the back door of the house. At first, we thought he maybe slipped and froze to death, but he had been hit on the back of the head."

"You need to get out of there as soon as possible," Brendan said.

"I can't just leave. There was a big storm yesterday and I don't know the condition of the roads. And besides, I came down in their car. If I insist on leaving now, they'll think I suspect them."

"Don't you?"

"What do you mean?"

"Do you know the relationship of Mr. and Mrs. Warren before his death? Is it possible that she may have killed him? They say poison is a woman's weapon."

"I heard you say that before. Whoever the 'they' is."

"He may have been having an affair. He may have been thinking of divorcing her. Who knows?"

"That doesn't seem likely if he changed his will to leave the property to her."

"Maybe he told her he was going to do that, and she took advantage of that knowledge."

"She seemed surprised when she heard it from the lawyer. Brendan, I don't like your suggestions."

"I'm sorry, I'm just trying to be objective. If there was marital discord it could have meant that Kitty was pulled into it. If her father were treating her mother badly, perhaps the daughter went to the rescue."

"No, I don't believe that at all. Not at all!"

"Is everything all right?" Kitty asked.

Amanda whirled around, unaware that she had been facing away from the stairway and hadn't heard her friend approach.

"Yes, fine. Fine," Amanda said, her hand over the mouthpiece. The she resumed her conversation with Brendan. "The sheriff has taken the housekeeper's son in for questioning."

"I think you need to either lock yourself in your room or be in the company of more than one person. That's the safest thing."

All that Amanda could think of was those movies where everyone is told to go to their room and lock the door. Just before the next person was murdered.

"I'm looking forward to the Policeman's Ball," Amanda said brightly to deflect Kitty's attention. "I hope you got the tickets already. Let me give you the number here so you can call tomorrow with an update." She rattled off the number, repeated it and said goodbye.

"Who was that?"

"Brendan. You know he's a police detective."

Kitty looked puzzled. "Yes. Obviously, I know he is. Were you calling him to come down here and sort things out?"

"I wish he could, but these folks are testy about their jurisdictions. He would have no authority here."

"Understandable, but this sheriff is out of his depth. All he can seem to do is bully people and make wild accusations."

"Do you think that Daniel could have killed August?"

"I don't know, but he couldn't have killed my father. He respected him too much. My father made sure that he got a decent lawyer. Usually in cases where the defendant can't pay, the judge assigns someone and they're usually the one attorney who's available. Meaning, not many clients, meaning, not successful."

"What a mess."

"My mother wants me to get some things from town. Come with me and we can stop for a proper lunch while we're at it."

The word of August's death had spread quickly and people in the dry goods store, as well as the nosy proprietor, stared at the two young women. They could feel the eyes of everyone on them as they paid and left.

"We're not going to the nice restaurant on Main Street. Everybody there knows me, and it will be the same cold shoulder and staring routine. Let's go to the diner toward the edge of town. The food's a bit greasy but we'll be anonymous."

As it was late morning but not yet lunchtime, there were few cars parked outside and whatever they were cooking made Amanda's stomach rumble.

"They do have good hamburgers and milkshakes here," Kitty said. She surveyed the space as they walked in and pronounced themselves safe from prying eyes. A waitress came to their booth with two glasses of water and took their order before going behind the counter and passing the slip into the kitchen through a hatchway.

No sooner had they settled in than an older waitress appeared and said, "Kitty? Kitty Warren?"

The look on Kitty's face was part recognition and part apprehension as she anticipated the barrage of questions.

"I'm Sally's mother."

"Oh, yes. Of course."

"I was so sorry to hear about your father."

"Thank you." While upset to be reminded of her loss, Kitty was relieved that the demise of August wasn't the topic of conversation. Not yet.

"I saw your father on the night he died. He had dinner here."

"Really?" That was a surprise to Kitty.

"He was with his brother and some other man who looked down whenever I came by as if he didn't want me to see him."

"Was it anyone you recognized?"

"He wasn't from around here. Strange looking fellow with fancy clothes if you know what I mean."

"I don't."

"One of those scarves around his neck and a pencil mustache. He scooted into the men's room just as I came by with the food."

There was a ding from the kitchen pass through.

"That's my order. Again, I'm awfully sorry. Please tell your mother."

"What do you make of that?" Amanda said.

"I don't know. But the sheriff probably never heard that information. And he never even searched August's room as far as I know. I think after our hearty meal, that's what we'll do."

"AUGUST ISN'T HERE," the landlady said to Kitty, after greeting her warmly. "Maybe he went back to Boston yesterday, although I don't know what the roads are like." There was a soft mewing noise and she reached into her apron pocket and pulled out a kitten.

The two young women cooed simultaneously. "He's so cute!"

Amanda held out her hands to pick up the tiny thing that showed its teeth as it vocalized.

"It's a she," the woman responded. "Her name is Marmalade."

"Marmie!" Kitty said taking the kitten out of Amanda's hands and burrowing her face in its neck. "Uncle Arthur asked me to come retrieve some papers he had left by mistake. We're going up to Boston tomorrow and we can bring them to him. How old is she?"

"Just a few weeks, I think. I had a sweet old cat, but she died recently. You'll never believe it, but she was poisoned."

Amanda and Kitty looked at each other briefly.

"Why anyone thinks there are rats in Hyannis, I don't know. But people put it down anyway with no consideration for other animals that could get to it like birds and my dear Millie."

"I'm sorry to hear that," Amanda said. "This tiny one will keep you company."

"She's going to be strictly an in-the-house cat. I'm not letting her out of my sight."

Kitty handed the kitten back to the landlady, who said, "My stars, it's getting late. I have some errands to do in town. I'll let you in and you can leave the key in my mailbox when you're done." She fished in her other apron pocket and produced a key and went back through her door.

Kitty opened the adjacent door to a large space with a bed in one corner, sofa and chairs adjacent and a desk.

"You certainly know how to tell a bald-faced lie," Amanda said, closing the door behind her.

"Practice," Kitty said.

"Let's take our time," Amanda said. "August is sounding more suspicious by the minute."

It wasn't that large of a room and neatly kept except for the books, magazines and papers stacked high on a desk. Even the chest of drawers next to it had receipts and cancelled checks in messy piles.

"He kept his room at the house considerably neater than this," Amanda said.

"That's because the room at the house was his shrine. A memento of his golden youth. It was all downhill from there."

"He was an architect, wasn't he? That's hardly going down in life."

"It shouldn't have been but somehow it was. He started at a prestigious firm, and they didn't make him a partner, so he went off on his own. It's hard to make a satisfying living designing additions to peoples' homes. Especially when they are your wealthy friends who balk at the prices that are charged."

"Nothing here," Amanda said, having searched under the bed and between the mattress and box spring. She went to the closet and put her hands in the pockets of the pants and suits that hung there without finding anything. She stood in front of the desk with her hands on her hips.

"Where would you hide something? If we're looking for a bottle, it's not going to be sitting under a pile of papers, is it?"

"I'm looking in the desk drawers anyway," Kitty said.

Amanda headed for the bathroom. She opened the medicine cabinet over the sink and took out each bottle in turn, opened it and then sniffed. She wasn't sure what arsenic smelled like or if it was even advisable to put her nose in a container, then decided just to read the label and shake the contents. A tin of Bayer aspirin looked like what sat in her medicine cabinet at home, and there was no mistaking the pink bottle of Pepto-Bismol for what it was. The other shelves held a razor, a shaving cup with a disk of soap in the bottom, iodine, Band-Aids, a bottle of hair tonic and toothpaste. She shut the mirrored door and spread open the shirred fabric that encircled the lower part of the sink. Nothing there but a wastebasket. She sighed.

Kitty was busy looking in the drawers when Amanda had a nagging thought. She went back to the area under the sink and felt around the enamel drainpipe but came away with nothing more than a dusty hand. No other hiding places were available in this sparse room, but out of curiosity, she opened the tank behind the toilet bowl and looked into the rusty bottom of the cistern expecting to find a bottle of some kind. Instead, she saw a wire hooked onto the back of the tank. Peering behind the tank she could just about make out something suspended from the wire.

"Kitty, I think I've found something."

Her friend came into the bathroom and saw the tank cover that had been removed. "He couldn't have put it in there," she said.

"No, behind it." Kitty craned her neck to look behind the tank. "How do we get it without it smashing onto the tiles?"

"Get a towel and put in on the floor in the back. In case I can't lift it up successfully, at least the towel should break its fall."

With a bath towel positioned on the tiles, Amanda gingerly lifted the wire up with the bottle suspended from it, banging the back of the tank.

"I've got it," she said, using a washcloth to pull it to safety so that her fingerprints would not be on the bottle. "Look. Most of the label has been scratched off but he couldn't fully get rid of the skull and crossbones. Whatever it is, it's poison."

Amanda was triumphant at her discovery but soon noticed that Kitty didn't share in the excitement.

"What's the matter?"

"You know I wasn't fond of my uncle, yet knowing he killed my father is a horrible thing to accept. What if there is tainted blood in our family?"

"Don't be ridiculous. There is no such thing. He and your father were brothers, and your father wasn't like that. We all choose our own path and either out of jealousy, greed or spite, he chose the wrong one. That's not who you are." Amanda gave Kitty a long hug.

"If August killed my father, then who killed August? You don't think it was my mother, do you?"

Chapter 23

Amanda and Kitty went directly to the sheriff's office and presented him with the bottle they had found in August's room.

"Careful," Amanda said, handing him the bottle still wrapped in a washcloth. "We don't want to get any other fingerprints on it." He gave her a withering look.

"You may have pointed to the murder of Rupert Warren, but that doesn't mean that I'm releasing Daniel for the death of August Warren."

Amanda had to admit to herself that he had a valid point. "You're welcome, by the way, for the discovery," she said aloud in an unpleasant tone.

A knock on the open door to the sheriff's office had a young officer standing and shifting from foot to foot. "There's someone here to see you."

"Who is it?" he snapped.

"Gertrude Robinson."

"Oh, I don't want to see her. She just wants to complain about me finding her son and locking him up."

"But there's more to tell," Gertrude said, appearing in the doorway. The officer slinked away, and she came into the room, nodded at the two young women and sat down with her handbag in her hand. "There's a lot more to tell."

"You two can go now," the sheriff said, shooing them away with his hand.

"They can stay," Gertrude said. And stay they did.

"It's not true that August was trying to get into the house and nobody heard him. He was already in the house for some time. I know because I let him in."

Amanda and Kitty exchanged looks.

"He was looking for something important he said, and he went up to the attic and rummaged around. I wasn't going to be caught having let him in after Mrs. Warren had Josiah to change the locks and all. I went up to the attic and gave him the key to the back door and told him to put it under the flowerpot next to the door when he was done. I could hear him walking around up above for some time and then I didn't hear anymore."

"What was he looking for?" the sheriff asked.

"The painting," Amanda said.

Everyone looked at her.

"What if that's the real painting that you found?" Amanda asked her friend.

"It can't be," Kitty said. "Your own notes about the investigation into the authenticity of the painting prove that he gave it to Scofield's Gallery."

"What if your uncle had a copy made and switched them out afterward at some time? Maybe he was going to sell it privately and keep the money for himself. There's every reason to believe that a Scofield buyer would see the provenance provided and believe it to be a real Turner. No one would be the wiser. He could benefit from it twice."

"Who the heck is Scofield?" the sheriff asked.

"A guy in fancy clothes with a pencil moustache," Amanda said. "With a lot on the line."

WHEN THEY GOT BACK to the house, Amanda asked to meet Kitty and her mother in the study while she rooted around in the bottom of her suitcase. She returned and handed a photograph to Mrs. Warren.

"Do you recognize this?"

"That's the Turner, but who is that?"

"Isn't that grandmother?" Kitty asked. "That dress in the attic was hers."

"It looks like a dress she had, but that's not her. I don't know who that is."

"What if that's someone August had pose in the dress to authenticate the ownership?"

"Why would he have to if everyone knew it was already in the family?"

"Maybe August tried too hard and that made Scofield suspicious. The gallery owner sensed something was wrong, otherwise why would he have got an attorney and had an investigation begun? But everything checked out. Then Scofield found out there had been a break in at the gallery, which led him to assume that someone had switched the paintings. He thought August now had the real one and he had been tricked. August hid it here when you were back in Boston. Later, he got back into the house with Gertrude's help and looked for the original where he had hidden it in the attic and gave up because Kitty had already discovered it and moved it to the study. I think that Scofield slipped in the house, knowing August had done something underhanded, took your sculpture but waited until August was outside to seek his revenge."

"That's quite a complicated setup," Mrs. Warren said.

"If you'll allow me to call Brendan in Boston, I can alert him to my theory, and he can find out Scofield's comings and goings for the past two weeks."

Amanda took longer than expected to lay out the entire scenario to Brendan, who confirmed through the department's paperwork that Scofield had reported a suspected break-in at his gallery but then called back almost immediately to say he was mistaken.

"That's when he realized that someone *had* broken in and knew it could only be August who came in to switch the paintings," Amanda said. "It seems Scofield wanted to get it back himself. But since August hadn't found it because it was in the study, Scofield didn't get it back either. They argued and well, you know what happened next."

"Good thinking. Convoluted, but a good solution. I'll take a ride over to his gallery and have a conversation with him."

"Remember that Caroline works there, and she would know when Scofield was in town and gone but don't ask her in front of her boss. I think we have a witness who saw both the

Warrens and Scofield shortly before Rupert was killed. Maybe both were involved."

"*We* have a witness?" Brendan asked.

"I consider it to be my first real case. If I can't become a police detective, then maybe I'll have to set up shop on my own."

There was silence on the other end of the line.

"Brendan? Are you still there?"

"I think we have a lot to talk about. When are you coming home?"

Chapter 24

It took two days before Brendan could verify Scofield's movements and while it was difficult to trace where he had been—except the dinner in the diner—he could prove that he hadn't been in Boston on either the night Rupert died, or the night August was killed. It meant Brendan going down to Hyannis and meeting with the sheriff and ingratiating himself as best he could so as not to seem to be stealing his case. After all, it would be up to the sheriff to arrest Scofield, although Brendan offered to assist.

"Now, explain that business about switching the paintings again?" the sheriff asked, flummoxed by the elaborate hoax. What became clear was that Daniel was not the murderer and that his mother's avowal that he was asleep in the next bed during the evening in question was the truth. One thing in Daniel's favor was that he had no knowledge of the artwork in the attic and, when told, was astonished at what an original Turner might be worth.

Follow up questions with several motel owners in nearby Barnstable confirmed that Scofield had been in the area the night Rupert was killed as well as the evening of August's demise. Whether he and August poisoned Rupert at the diner that evening, or Arthur acted alone, they were not able to find out immediately as Scofield clammed up and summoned an attorney. To Amanda's relief, it was not anyone in her father's firm since they didn't specialize in criminal defense.

Amanda returned to Boston with Brendan, happy to be in his calm presence and hear about all the details of the Policeman's Ball scheduled to take place the night before Christmas Eve, only two days away.

"Tell me all about the band and the general schedule of things," she said.

"There will be real cocktails this year for a change. Then we'll be seated for dinner. Table for eight."

"Who's at our table?"

"Dominick and his date," he paused to build up the tension. "Your Miss Bailey."

"No! What happened to his girlfriend?"

"She wanted to get married, and he said he wasn't ready, so she went off and got engaged to someone else. To be honest, I think he was relieved."

"She didn't seem to approve of his profession, although it's a good one with a pension, too."

Brendan shrugged. "I think her fiancé is in the trades. It may be what she was used to, not someone with odd hours dealing with criminals."

"Who else is at our table?"

"The Assistant Chief and his wife."

"That sounds impressive."

"He's a good fellow and maybe, just maybe, if the Chief ever retires, he will take his place. A straight shooter."

"And?"

"The Assistant District Attorney and his wife."

Amanda was impressed by the group Brendan had assembled. "But he's not a policeman."

"Of course not. But the prosecutors always want to stick close to the police, and the opportunity of being seen in a social setting and contributing to the Police Welfare Fund never hurts."

"Especially if he is looking to be the District Attorney at some point in the near future."

"Exactly."

"Brendan, I did miss you." She slid over to snuggle against his shoulder in the car.

"And I missed you. Tell me what slinky dress you will be wearing."

"You'll see," she teased him.

The night of the ball, Louisa helped her sister get dressed in the gown she had designed especially for her. It was raspberry-colored velvet with a deep V-neck, ruffled half-sleeves, a defined waist and mermaid hem.

"It's stunning," Amanda said. "You really are an artist."

"Thank you," Louisa said. "Do you think Mother could lend you a necklace?"

Amanda pursed her lips in concentration. "I've met Brendan's colleagues but only in work situations. I don't want to overdo it at a social function. I'm in a quandary."

"Your hair looks terrific, your makeup subtle yet alluring. I have just the thing," Louisa said, disappearing for a few minutes. She returned with a black satin ribbon and tied it around her sister's neck. "What do you think?"

"Perfect!" Amanda said. It set off her complexion and added panache to the already striking dress without overdoing things. They heard the doorbell ring and giggled a bit, knowing that the man of the hour had arrived. Nonetheless, they waited until Simona came up to tell her that Mr. Halloran had arrived before Amanda went down the stairs with Louisa trailing behind.

The look on Brendan's face said everything. He was in awe, he was delighted, he was in love.

"You look terrific," he said, kissing her on the cheek.

"Have a wonderful time, you two," Louisa said.

"Where are your parents?" Brendan asked. "I was hoping to see them."

"Another Christmas party. But they'll be home by the time the ball is over, and you can see them then."

"Good idea."

Amanda admired Brendan's evening clothes she had seen him in before and they suited him, bringing out the dark gleam of his hair and accentuating his blue eyes. He helped her into the long evening coat, and they walked into the sharp evening air arm in arm.

Brendan looked up at the clear, starry sky. "What a wonderful night this will be."

Amanda snuggled into his arm and once in the car, he turned on the ignition and the heat but did not put it into gear right away.

"What's next?" he asked her.

"You mean after the ball?"

"I mean with work or not work. Have you given any thought to it?"

"Actually, I have. I've already talked with my father about it a bit and I'm going to take over the investigator role at his law firm."

Brendan turned in surprise. "Well, that's an interesting turn of events."

"Not to brag, but I was able to figure out the business with the Warren family, the painting and Scofield. I do have a curious mind and am dogged about following clues."

"True," he said.

"I might also want to get a private investigator's license." She waited for his reaction.

"Really? Are you sure you want to do that kind of work? It can be gritty and messy and dangerous."

Amanda faced him. "I know, but haven't I been doing that already? And I'm wonderfully positioned by having an important connection in the police force."

"And who might that be?" he asked.

"Who do you think?" she said, giving him a kiss. "I did miss kissing you."

"I will absolutely not stand in your way of whatever direction your work life takes you, but I do have one requirement."

Amanda pulled back in concern.

Brendan fished in his pocket and pulled out a small box. "Your Christmas present."

"Two days early?" she said in a teasing tone. But when she opened the box and saw a diamond engagement ring, her tone changed. "Oh, Brendan. I don't know. Can we do this?"

"What do you mean? Of course, we can! I have my work, you have yours, I like your family, my family likes you—what stands in the way?"

Amanda could think of many things that would stand in the way, but they were trivial compared to how she felt about him.

"Nothing. Nothing at all! Let's go to the ball so I can show off my ring and my fiancé."

They laughed and kissed, and he put the car in gear and drove away.

Stay tuned: there will be more mysteries for Amanda Burnside to solve when she takes on the role of private investigator.

But for now, let's jump ahead to the future. Meet **Gemma Farnese,** a contemporary amateur sleuth who becomes embroiled in a murder in her workplace.
Find it here:
A MURDER IN THE PRIMATE LAB

Sign up for my newsletter for more titles:

www.Andreas-books.com
If you enjoyed this book, please let other readers know.
Reviews help readers discover my books, so feel free to leave a
short line or two:
MY REVIEW PAGE

Thank you! Happy Reading,
Andrea

Printed in Great Britain
by Amazon

8aaf7b1a-71b4-4959-9fbd-8f605b04441bR01